WEDDING BELLS AND HOODOO SPELLS

SAGE'S WEDDING

MELISSA F. MILLER

BROWN STREET BOOKS

Print ISBN 978-1-940759-46-3

CHAPTER 1

Sage

𝒥'm getting married in three weeks. I have no flowers, no music, and, as of today, no one to officiate the ceremony. It sounds pretty bad—and it is—but at least I've got a cake. At least, I *think* I've got a cake.

I paw through my purse and dig out my cell phone to call the baker, who just happens to be my older sister Rosemary.

"Sage, hi! Are you getting excited?"

Her cheerful voice is like a knife to my gut. I always imagined the weeks leading up to my wedding as a time of romance and elegance—like my regular life, only with a golden, soft filter applied to it. And while I'm definitely excited about marrying Roman, my actual wedding ... that's shaping up to be a disaster.

"Yeah," I manage weakly. "I just want to make sure we're all set for the cake."

The background din of pots and pans banging together and echoing off the tile walls of Rosemary's commercial kitchen stops. She's silent for a long moment.

"You don't think I'd let you down on your wedding cake, do you?" Her voice is dangerously soft.

"No!"

It's true. I don't think so. But I also didn't think that Reverend Walker would flake. Or that every band and DJ within a seventy-five-mile radius would be unavailable. Or that the flower shop would lose my contract and the florist would look straight in my eyes and claim to have no memory of meeting with me to pick out centerpieces and bouquets.

I never imagined *any* of these events would come to pass, but here I am. So Rosemary's firstborn sense of responsibility and obligation notwithstanding, I thought I better check.

My answer must satisfy her, because the clattering resumes. "Okay. Hey, I talked to Thyme yesterday. We're going to fly out there this weekend and take you to this amazing spa that Muffy recommended."

I shake my head as if she can see me.

"Nuh-uh. No way. First of all, if Muffy Moore likes the place, it's probably crazy expensive—"

"It's our treat."

I keep going. "*And* I don't have time for a spa day."

"That's exactly why you need one. You can't run yourself down before the wedding. You can take a couple hours for yourself to hang out with your sisters and just relax."

I really can't, but I also recognize Rosemary's will-brook-no-argument voice and don't have the energy to take her on.

"Sounds great," I chirp, making a mental note to call Thyme later and see if I can wheedle my younger sister into canceling the plans, so I don't have to.

"Excellent. I can't tell you how much I'm looking forward to it. My little sister's going to be a married woman in less than a month," she muses.

Maybe. If my luck turns around.

She interrupts the scene of impending doom that's playing out in my mind. "Have you talked to Mom and Dad?"

I sigh. Mom and Dad. My list of potential wedding day disasters wouldn't be complete without the reminder that my incarcerated parents may not be able to secure a day pass to attend.

"I did. Agent Morgan is still trying to pull some strings to get them released for the wedding. But Mom says if they can't be there, just make sure we record it."

She drops her voice and asks gently, "Is that why you sound so stressed out? They'll be there, Sage. If they can, they'll be there."

In my heart, I know she's right. And, while under ordinary circumstances, the chance that my parents might miss my wedding would probably be my main concern, I haven't really had time to worry about it. Mom and Dad are serving sentences for tax evasion. If they can't be there, it'll be because of some bureaucratic hold up and, well, their own bad behavior. The outcome is literally out of my hands.

But everything else? Everything else is on me. I'm supposed to be making things happen so I can have a beautiful ceremony and reception. Meanwhile, I feel like my hair is on fire, and I can't find any water. My convict parents are the least of my worries.

Rosemary waits a beat.

"I don't want to rush you off the phone, but I need to get these quiches in the oven. Dave and I are going to look at a house this afternoon."

She and Detective Dave got married just over a year ago, and they've already moved fully into the grown-up world of home-ownership, mortgage applications, and meetings with realtors. Meanwhile, I have one free weekday a week to come over from the island where I live and work as a nanny to pull this wedding together, and I can't even get anyone to return my phone calls.

"I can't believe it!" I squeal, my excitement for her momentarily overtaking my misery. "Good luck."

She reminds me to pull up the website with the spa's list of services so we can pick our treatments, and we say our goodbyes.

I drop my phone into my purse as I round the corner to the dress shop where I'm having my gown fitted and reach for the door. It's locked.

I peer inside. Jessalyn's Dress Shoppe is closed up and dark. Confused, I check my watch, even though it's eleven o'clock in the morning, and I'm right on time for my appointment.

An index card taped to the door catches my eye. Someone's scribbled a hurried note: *Closed indefinitely due to family emergency.*

I lean my forehead against the glass and whimper, "My wedding is cursed."

~

"YOUR WEDDING IS CURSED."

I lean in closer to Roman's grandmother, sure I've misheard her.

"Pardon?"

She nods her head, swallows a spoonful of gumbo, and repeats herself, "I said, you've been cursed." She gives me a watery smile before resuming her attack on her bowl of food.

I sit in silence, trying to formulate a response to the octogenarian's announcement that my wedding's been cursed, and come up blank.

Beside me, Roman must sense my befuddlement. He pats my thigh reassuringly under the white tablecloth and grins at his grandmother. "Now, Granny Effie, don't go teasing my bride-to-be like that," he scolds her good-naturedly.

Any trace of amusement vanishes from the woman's wrinkled face and her spoon clatters to the table. She plants both elbows on the table, juts her chin forward, and locks eyes with her grandson.

"You listen good, Roman. This isn't a laughing matter. Y'all have been cursed. And you need to take heed, or it's only gonna get worse."

She stares at him for a long moment before picking up her spoon and returning to her lunch.

I focus on the tablecloth's floral pattern, losing myself in the dizzying swirls and curlicues. She's joking, I reassure myself firmly. Or, sadly, maybe she's slipping into dementia, blurring reality and fantasy. It happens.

But I can't ignore the clench of my stomach, like a tight fist in my belly, or the way my pulse crashes against my throat like a breaking wave.

I wait until Roman's in the restroom, which in reality is just his move to intercept the check before the waitress brings it to the table and Effie insists on paying. They do this little endearing dance every week. Last week, Effie outsmarted him and slipped the waitress some cash when she brought the sweet teas—a little prepayment of sorts. So this week, she'll let her grandson win. It's only sporting.

This is my chance. I lean toward her and drop my voice conspiratorially.

"Ms. Lyman—"

"Sugar, I know I told you to call me Granny Effie. You're as good as family." She pats my cheek.

"Granny Effie, am I though? I'm worried the wedding may not happen after all ...." I have to pause here and consider how ridiculous what I'm about to say sounds. "I mean, if it's cursed like you say."

She nods with satisfaction. "I'm glad to see one of you has the sense to take this seriously. Now, don't fret too much, I believe he only cursed the wedding itself, not your union. That's a small blessing."

"He? You know who did this?"

Did what? My rational brain taunts me. *You can't really think some spell is responsible for all the problems you're running into.*

I ignore the voice inside my head and focus on the old woman. She purses her mouth in a little bow and twitches it from side to side, considering what and how much to tell me.

"Granny, please hurry. Before Roman comes back." I'm pleading now, but I don't care. I need to know what she's talking about.

She's apparently made up her mind. She squares her jaw and says, "We Lymans have had a long-running feud, for ages and ages, with a powerful family of conjurers, the Davises. It started before my time. Even as a wee little girl I can remember my papa telling me to stay away from the Davis Family. He said they had strong, dark magic."

Her faded eyes stare out at the bustling restaurant but I can tell she's seeing something else, something far away and long ago. I reach for her hand.

She gives my hand a surprisingly strong squeeze and goes on. "I was just a slip of a girl, and, of course, I didn't pay my papa any mind. I was fascinated by the idea of magic, even dark magic. So one Sunday after church, I raced away through the field that separated our property from the Davises' place and sneaked into their barn to look around."

Her quavering voice is hypnotic. Despite the fact that I know full well I'm an adult woman sitting in a bright and busy restaurant, my heart hammers like I'm a small child crouched in the shadows of a creepy old barn, spying on a sinister adult.

"What happened?"

A sly half-smile dances across her lips and she sips what's left of her tea, which, from the looks of it, is mostly undissolved sugar. My teeth ache just watching her.

"If he saw me, he never let on. But, looking back, he must've known I was there. He put on quite a show, hollerin' and dancin' barefoot around a cauldron—"

"Wait. There was a *cauldron* in the barn? What kind of barn has a cauldron lying around?"

"Well, now, it might've been a kettle, if you're gonna be fussy about the details. Or maybe a barrel. But, to me, that day, it was a cauldron." She crosses her arms and gives me a defiant stare.

"Sure, I'm sorry for interrupting. Please, go on."

"He did a lot of wavin' his hands and callin' on the spirits to punish the Lymans."

Despite myself, I gasp. "He said that?"

"Clear as day. It scared the bejeezus out of me. I waited until he went into the tack room for something and took off running as fast as my legs would carry me. I was slick with sweat and my Sunday dress was covered in hay and dirt when I got home. My mama was madder than a hornet." She chuckles at the memory.

"I'll bet you were in big trouble."

"You'd a thought I'd get a switching. But she took one look at my face and must've known something was wrong. She drew me a bath and put me to bed even though it was still daylight. But that wasn't the end of it."

"It wasn't?"

She shakes her head. "I woke up the next morning running a high fever. I was covered head to toe with itchy red bumps and my throat, oh, it ached."

My eyes widen. "Really?"

"A-yup. My daddy went into town to get the doctor, who said I had scarlet fever and had to be isolated from the family. He said there wasn't anything he could do, and if I was strong enough I'd live. Well, as soon as he left I broke down bawling and confessed to my mama about where I'd been and what I'd seen in the barn."

I'm on the edge of my seat, but it occurs to me that Roman's taking an unusually long time in the bathroom. Although, to be fair, he *did* drink about a gallon of that sweet tea. I can't very well ask Granny Effie to speed up her story of her brush with death, but I do really want to hear the whole tale. So I clamp my mouth shut so as not to interject and nod enthusiastically.

"Mama started wailin' and cryin' that I'd been cursed. She sent my brother to fetch the root woman. That woman took one look at me and boiled some holly leaves with pine tar and told me to drink it in the morning and midday. Then she told Mama to make sassafras root tea and have me drink that in the afternoon and night. Finally, she mixed up a poultice of clay and who knows what and plopped it down on my chest. She said that'd lift the curse right off me. And do ya' know what?"

I'm leaning so far forward that I'm in danger of tipping over and faceplanting into my plate of okra and rice. "What?" I breathe.

"I was up runnin' around with my brothers and sisters by the middle of the week." She settles back in her chair with a satisfied smile just as Roman returns to the table.

He rests a hand on my shoulder. "Are my two favorite ladies ready to go?"

"Why don't you be a good boy and bring the car around?" she reaches up and pats his arm.

Effie's stubborn insistence that she can walk as well as anybody is legend, so the request throws him for a loop.

"Are you feeling okay, Granny?" His brow is a maze of worried furrows.

"Right as rain. I'm just wearing the wrong shoes." She lies fluidly.

His forehead relaxes, and he drops a kiss beside my ear before trotting off.

Once he's out of earshot, she considers me carefully. "You think I'm crazy, don't ya?"

I laugh. Effie doesn't know about my hippie-dippie upbringing. I'd be the last person in the world to dismiss the power of natural remedies.

"Because the root woman's potions worked when the doctor had nothing to offer? Not in the least," I assure her.

She gives me a half-smile, then her eyes narrow shrewdly. "But you don't think the curse is real." It's a statement, not a question.

I answer honestly. "I'm not sure what I think. You said this curse has been hanging over the family for ages, right?"

"Sure as shooting."

"Why don't you tell me more about it while we wait at the front for Roman?"

I stand and extend my hand to help her to her feet. She swats it away.

"There's not enough time to tell you every misfortune that's befallen us because of the hex, but I'll give you the highlights."

As we wend our way through the restaurant, she draws a deep breath and starts ticking off disasters. "There was the fire of 1948, Uncle Jerome's bankruptcy twelve years later, that awful car accident that took young Marlin …."

CHAPTER 2

Thyme

*M*y phone chirps obnoxiously and I jump in my chair.

Crap, crap, crap.

I reach for my bag, which is sitting on the floor under my desk, and scrabble one-handed through the contents until I find the thing. I fumble with the buttons while my ringtone blares. Finally, I manage to silence the thing. My face burns, and I glance at the people around me, expecting to see rolled eyes and glares. But nobody appears to notice, including the professor speaking at the front of the class.

Maybe noisy cell phones aren't the faux pas they were five years ago when I was an undergrad?

I surreptitiously place the phone in my lap and check my notifications. I have a series of texts and one missed call from Sage. It's my own fault she's bothering me in the middle of this lecture. It's lunchtime, and I don't usually have personal training clients now. It's always been a great time of day for my sisters to reach me.

I haven't told either of them that I'm taking classes part-time to finish my graduate degree in psychology. My boyfriend thinks the secrecy is weird. But Victor doesn't understand: my older sisters have their own, grown-up lives now. Rosemary's a newly-wed, and Sage is planning her wedding. I want something that's mine and only mine. It feels delicious to have a secret.

Besides, I'm not even sure what I plan to do with this degree. I always thought that, once the three of us got out from under the mountain of debt burdening the resort we co-own, I'd go back to school, get my Ph.D., and become a research psychologist. It turns out, though, that I actually like working with my clients as a yoga and Pilates personal trainer. Maybe I can use my under-standing of human psychology to motivate people, not only to exercise, but to live better, more fulfilling lives overall?

It's just a vague idea right now, but it won't come to anything if I don't pass this class—which I'm *not* going to do if I don't pay attention. So I shove the phone back in my bag and return my focus to the lecture on the chemical basis of memory. Whatever Sage wants can wait. She's probably just trying to coordinate our upcoming spa weekend.

I forget about the phone and my quarter-life crisis and manage to focus for the rest of the class.

I finally read the texts while waiting in line for my smoothie at the student union:

Sage: My wedding's cursed.

Sage: Are you there?

Sage: I'm serious, Thyme. What am I gonna do?

Cursed? I stifle a giggle and text a laughing emoji.

Me: :D

Three little dots appear on the screen; she's already responding.

Sage: It's not funny.

She can't be serious. But, maybe she's having second thoughts? I start to type 'if you're not ready, you don't have to do this' but shake my head and delete the words.

She loves Roman, and I know she's ready for this commitment. So what gives?

I stare down at my phone, trying to formulate a response, until the guy in line behind me taps me on the shoulder. "Hey, lady, your smoothie is ready."

He points to the counter while I process the fact that being in my mid-twenties qualifies me for *hey, lady* treatment.

A harassed-looking teenager wearing a paper hat drums her fingers on the counter, waiting for me to pick up my drink.

"Oh, sorry. Thanks." I grab the smoothie and make a big show of stuffing a few dollars into the tip jar then maneuver my way to a quiet corner where I can deal with Sage's bizarre texts. I sip my avocado-berry-mint concoction and type with my thumbs:

Me: Is everything okay?

Sage: No. everything's not okay. I TOLD you, I'm cursed!

I can almost hear her voice going up an octave. I hurriedly respond:

Me: Do you need to borrow some money?

Sage: No, I need someone to lift the curse.

Again with the curse. My sisters and I have all been under a lot of stress the past few years, so I have to entertain the possibility she's had a break with reality. My mind turns to Skylar and Dylan. Sage takes care of the children of a professional golfer while his wife does whatever rich ladies do. I need to make sure those kids are okay.

Me: Are you at work?

Sage: No. Muffy's giving me Wednesdays off to plan the wedding. You know, the one that's currently under a curse.

I open a new text screen and message Rosemary:

Me: Have you talked to Sage lately?

Just like Sage, Rosemary responds instantly:

Rosemary: Yes, this morning. She was weird. Call you later. Can't talk now. I'm with realtor.

A girl with an enormous backpack pulling her off balance jostles me, and I nearly lose my drink.

"Sorry, ma'am," she calls over her shoulder as she lurches away and I bobble the smoothie.

First lady, now ma'am? I've had enough of this place and decide to finish my text conversation and my sorry excuse for lunch outside in the courtyard. I weave through the crowds and find a spot on a stone bench. Then I pull open the text thread with Rosemary.

Me: Happy house hunting. Call me when you can. I think Sage may have had a nervous breakdown. Should I ask Roman to check on her?

My anxiety ratchets up while I wait for a response. When it comes, I spew smoothie all over the sidewalk.

Sage: I have NOT had a nervous breakdown, thank you very much. I need HELP but I can see that you're not going to help me. Screw you, and Rosemary, too.

Argh! Misdirected texts are the bane of my existence. You'd think I'd have learned after I accidentally texted my boyfriend Victor's grandfather about my killer cramps, but apparently not. (Luckily Papa Jorge only reads Portuguese.)

Now, I've lost my appetite, so I toss what's left of the drink into the nearest trash receptacle and try to call Sage. I'm not surprised when the call rolls to voicemail. I leave a message begging for forgiveness and telling her how much I'm looking forward to our spa day. I ask her to please call me and promise to take her seriously.

It's the best I can do, so I stow the phone back in my bag and head for the subway. I can't shake my worries about Sage. Luckily, my final client of the day is a yoga shred devotee; so, if nothing else, I should be able to sweat out my bad feelings before I meet Victor to see his friend perform in an off-off-off-off-off-(just one off short of the production ending up in New Jersey)-Broadway play.

I make a note to ask Rosemary to call Sage again, too. That's the benefit of having two sisters. When one of us steps in it with a sister, we can call on the other to help us clean up the mess.

And I seem to have made a mighty mess of things with Sage.

CHAPTER 3

Rosemary

*a*fter viewing the condo—which somehow manages to be both way too tiny and way too expensive—I drop Dave off at the station. Then I take Mona Lisa for a long walk so we can both soak up the glorious Los Angeles weather. Once I've had a full dose of sunshine, I find a shady spot in the doggie park and plop down on a bench to give Sage a call. After all, I did promise Thyme. And I hate when people don't do what they say they will.

As I reach for my phone, I rethink the wisdom of this plan. If Sage really is as upset as Thyme says she is, my calling to check on her is liable to set her off. I hesitate for a nanosecond before pulling up her fiancé's number instead.

I don't know Roman all that well. That's one of the downsides of living clear on the other side of the country from my sisters. I don't see them—or the men in their lives—as much as I'd like. And when Sage, Thyme, and I *do* see each other, we're almost always looking to spend some uninterrupted sister time together.

Still, I like Roman a lot. For one thing, he adores my sister.

We're talking maybe a half-step away from worship. For another, he's a very sensible and grounded person. Which is not to say that Sage isn't, because she is. But having just planned my own wedding a little over a year ago, I haven't forgotten how frantic those last weeks were. It's no surprise she's stressed and acting flighty.

"Hi, this is Roman," a deep, mellifluous voice fills my ear and shakes me out of my rumination.

"Hi, it's Rosemary ... Field, er, Drummond," I add belatedly in case he knows a bunch of Rosemarys.

"Sure. I thought I recognized your number. Is everything okay?"

"I was hoping you could tell me that."

"Excuse me?"

"Thyme and I are a little bit worried about Sage. She seems ... out of sorts?" I'm not exactly sure how to describe her state of mind without sounding melodramatic.

He blows out a long, loud breath that turns into a sigh. "Oh, man. This is all my grandmother's fault."

"Umm ..." I stammer, too baffled to say much else.

"See, I take my Granny Effie out for lunch at her favorite Lowcountry restaurant once a week, and she just loves it when I bring Sage along." He pauses.

"I don't think this has anything to do with your grandmother—"

"Yeah, actually, it does. Granny Effie has gotten it into Sage's head that our wedding's been hexed."

"Hexed?" I repeat dumbly.

"Oh, right, sorry. Cursed, jinxed, the victim of bad juju. Down here folks believe in spirits. Good ones and bad ones." A defensive edge creeps into his voice.

I hurry to reassure him. "You're talking to a woman who grew up leaving offerings for the fairies in the garden and searching with her sisters for sprites, elves, and goblins in the woods. So I may not know what precisely the Gullah/Geechee believe, but I'd never judge anyone's belief in natural spirits. Neither would Sage or Thyme."

He mutters something I can't quite make out.

"Could you say that again?"

"I'm just thinking out loud. I wonder if that's why Sage is so susceptible to Granny Effie's tomfoolery?"

Judging by his tone, Roman didn't spend *his* childhood hunting for the elementals. He might well think his granny is off her rocker, he just doesn't want *me* to think it. Got it. Glad I didn't tell him about the summer we met that selkie on the beach.

For the record, I don't *still* believe in spirits, and I'm pretty sure Thyme doesn't either.

But Sage? Let's just say she always was the most enthusiastic about our mom's stories of magical creatures. Even so, I suspect there's a more mundane explanation for her current goofiness.

"It's possible the stress of planning the wedding is getting to Sage." I click my tongue and wonder too late whether it's impolite to tell the groom that the wedding plans are driving his bride-to-be bananas.

He doesn't seem to take offense. "I just wish Granny had never brought it up. Sage is convinced every little thing that goes wrong is because of some ancient curse."

"What sorts of little things are going wrong?" As interesting as the curse sounds, I'm pretty sure we need to keep the focus on the here and now.

He exhales, "Uh … let's see. We don't have flowers, the band canceled, her dressmaker went out of town and isn't returning calls. Just stuff like that."

I bite down hard on my lower lip to keep from pointing out that enough *stuff like that* adds up to one freaking disaster of a wedding.

It's no wonder Sage is panicking. And it makes a weird kind

of sense that she's glommed onto the idea of a curse to explain away her string of bad luck.

"Don't worry," I reassure him. "Thyme and I are coming in this weekend. We'll get her mind off the madness and help her get the wedding back on track."

"I hope so. I've never seen her like this before." His voice wobbles with worry.

"Planning a wedding alters a person's brain chemistry. I can speak with authority on this. It's nothing to worry about; Sage'll be back to normal as soon as you say your vows."

"Isn't it pregnancy that messes up brain chemistry?"

"It's the same scientific mechanism," I inform him. This is a baseless statement, in that there's no, you know, *science* behind it. But my lived experience tells me it's true all the same.

"Huh. Well, you'd know—after all, you're the scientist."

Actually, I'm the organic caterer. But, once upon a time, I was a chemist. But, again, I'm not relying on anything I learned in a laboratory or a lecture hall to support my assertion. I'm relying on the fact that, when *I* was planning *my* wedding, I managed to get abducted by a local gangster who stashed me in a storage unit (wearing my wedding dress) with my estranged, on-the-lam parents. It's a long story. But, yeah, it's safe to say a bride-to-be's brain can go a little haywire in that final stretch before the big day.

"Trust me. Sage will pull herself together. Do me a favor and don't mention this conversation to her, okay?" I hold my breath, hoping he's not the type to protest he would never keep secrets from the woman he loves.

Sure, as a general rule, open communication is a solid life choice. But Sage is already mad at Thyme and me—a smidge of discretion's in order here.

He lets loose a long, rumbling laugh. "Don't you worry about that. Do you have any idea how much trouble I'd be in with Sage if she found out I was telling tales to her sister? I don't need to bring that hellfire down on myself. No, ma'am, I surely don't."

"Glad we're on the same page. Just humor her on the curse stuff for now. Thyme and I will help her get everything straightened out this weekend."

"Thanks. Just don't forget, you ladies are supposed to be getting pampered, too."

"Don't worry. We'll leave her refreshed, relaxed, and ready to take on the world—and that includes the supernatural world."

"I'm gonna hold you to that, now." The tension's left his voice, and I end the call feeling very satisfied with myself.

I thumb out a text to Thyme:

> **Me:** Spoke to Roman. No worries. S has NOT had a mental breakdown. She's just stressed out. Planning is spiraling out of control. We'll help her this weekend. Everything is FINE. :-)

Sometimes being the oldest sister who needs to solve all the problems can be a bit exhausting, but, at the end of the day, I'm glad my sisters and I are so close.

We'll whip Sage's wedding into shape and spend the rest of the weekend drinking mimosas, getting facials, and having our nails done. Shoot, if we get her plans straightened out fast enough, I'm going to book myself a hot stone massage.

I lean back, close my eyes, and let the sun's warmth wash over my face. Yeah, a hot stone massage is definitely in order.

CHAPTER 4

Sage

*A*fter the conversation with Roman's grandmother fades from the forefront of my mind, I start to calm down and feel a little bit silly about my frantic texts to Thyme.

That's not to say I completely rule out the possibility of a curse—because I don't. I'm not someone who dismisses unexplained natural phenomena out of hand. You can thank (or blame) my mom for that. When we were growing up, she was big on magic and spirits. If you ask her, she'll tell you it was great for three little girls to live in a world rich with imagination and fantasy.

And it was.

The problem is, it wasn't all make-believe to me, not the way it was for Rosemary and Thyme. I realize this sounds sort of silly, but one of the reasons I like working with little kids is I think they have better vision than adults. They see things that are invisible to us; they hear things that are inaudible to us; they feel things that we shrug off as a breeze or *déjà vu* or whatever.

Maybe part of it is a deliberate leaving behind of childish

things, like imaginary friends and magic, as people get older, but I don't think that's all of it. I have this theory that just as vision fades and hearing degrades as we age, our innate ability to sense the otherworldly wanes as part of a natural progression.

So, long story short, do I think spirits exist? Yes.

Do I think some creepy conjurer has slapped a curse on my wedding with Roman? Umm ... probably not? But I'd sure like to know more about this man and the feud between the two families.

I decide doing some research will put my mind at ease. So I scrap my plan to spend the rest of my day off scrambling to make contingency arrangements for all the pieces of my wedding that are falling apart. I figure I can start by talking to Roman's relatives. With any luck, I'll learn some family history, satisfy my curiosity, and prove there's no curse.

There's no reason to let Roman know about my plans. He'll just try to convince me I'm being ridiculous. And as for Rosemary and Thyme, those two can kiss my bony butt if they don't want to be supportive. Unless the "Bridezilla" marathon I watched that one weekend lied to me, bridesmaids are supposed to give in to the bride's unreasonable demands and whims. I know my sisters are probably talking about me behind my back this very minute, but I brush that thought off, raise my chin, and point my car toward Roman's Auntie Denise's place. I'm filled with resolve and hope.

This new, calm approach to the whole situation lasts approximately ten minutes.

I'm not even halfway to Denise's house when my cell phone rings. I glance at the display before answering. I'm in no mood to talk to either of my sisters right now.

It's Roman's number, so I pick up the call.

"Hey, what's up? Aren't you supposed to be working with Chip?"

I know Roman's on the other end because I hear him breathing, hard and fast. But he's not saying a word.

My pulse starts to hammer like crazy and my stomach drops. I can just tell something's wrong.

"Roman? Are you okay?"

"You're not going to believe this," he finally says in a tone of voice that does nothing to settle my nerves.

"Are you hurt?"

"No."

"What happened?"

He clears his throat. "After I took Granny home, I stopped by the jewelry store. The jeweler called yesterday to say the rings were in, so I ran in and picked them up on my way to meet Chip at the club."

"Uh-huh. He wanted to work on his short game, right?"

"Yeah. So I left the ring boxes in my glove compartment. I locked up the car and everything, but, I mean ... it's the freaking country club. I didn't think for a second that they wouldn't be safe."

A sick certainty washes over me. "The rings are gone?"

"I don't even understand how. Nothing else is missing. And the doors are still locked. How'd they even get in? And who would break into a VW bug in the first place? You know the club, the lot's full of BMWs, Ferraris, and Bentleys. Why bother with *my* crappy car?"

It's the curse.

The words spring to mind instantly but I bite them back. Saying it out loud isn't going to help anything. Before I can think of a better response, he's talking again.

"Anyway, I've already talked to the insurance guy, and I'm waiting for the police department to send an officer over to take my statement. I just wanted you to know I might be late picking you up. I don't know how long this is gonna take."

"Picking me up for what?"

"Ballroom dancing class, remember?"

I didn't, actually. Our dance lesson completely slipped my mind after I decided to research the curse.

"Right, right. Well, I'm actually on my way to your Aunt Denise's house for a short visit. Why don't I just meet you at the studio after I leave there?"

"Okay. Wait, what are you doing out at Aunt Denise's?"

"Umm … wedding stuff."

I figure he's sufficiently distracted by the missing rings that he's not going to press me for details, and he doesn't.

"Oh. Okay. So I'll see you later."

We exchange I love yous and I end the call.

I jam my foot down on the gas pedal and tear off in the direction of Denise's place like I'm being chased by a pack of hellhounds—or at least one evil spirit with an agenda.

I'M NOT GONNA LIE, Roman's aunt intimidates me more than a little. Denise is a force of nature shoved into a five-foot-two-inch perfectly coiffed and manicured package. Every time I've seen her, her hat has matched her suit dress and her shoes have matched her fingernail polish. (And yes, that means what you think it does—she's always dressed to the nines, even if she's just doing her grocery shopping.)

Denise Lyman brings that same careful, detailed attention that she devotes to her appearance to every other aspect of her life. She's not only put together, she's a take-charge gal. I can't even begin to tell you how many church committees and ladies organizations she runs. And she's the reason Roman has his job and ever got to know his father. In short, she's a warm, expressive woman who doesn't pull her punches. So, the way I see it, she's my best bet at getting to the truth about the feud between the Lymans and the Davises.

As I pull into the driveway in front of her immaculate cottage, she looks up from pruning her flower bushes and gives me a surprised but delighted smile and an enthusiastic wave. I note that her gardening gloves match her sunhat. By the time I'm out of the car, both gloves and hat have been neatly set aside on her potting bench. She removes a coordinating apron and folds it precisely. Then she grabs me by the shoulders and pulls me in for a tight hug.

"Child, this is the nicest surprise. And don't you have just the best timing? I've been waiting on a fresh-baked red velvet cake to cool. Let's go inside. You can have a glass of tea and keep me company while I frost it."

I trail her inside and realize I've yet to get a word in edgewise. I wait until she takes a breath and offer to help her frost her cake. She waves me off and ties yet another apron around her waist as I situate myself at her highly polished oak kitchen table.

She bangs around in the refrigerator for half a minute then hands me a glass of sweet tea. I smile weakly, brace myself for the sugar assault, and wonder for the eight thousandth time how anyone south of the Mason-Dixon manages to have any teeth.

"What brings you out this way? I didn't expect to see you until choir practice tomorrow."

See, this is a perfect example of how Denise operates. I must've told her a dozen times that I'm not comfortable singing in public, but somehow she interpreted that as a burning desire to sing second soprano in the church choir and signed me up. I dread every rehearsal, but I'm glad she's brought up the subject of church because it gives me an opening.

"Did you know Reverend Walker isn't going to be able to marry me and Roman?" I say in a casual tone as she beats an inordinate amount of powdered sugar and a brick of cream cheese together in a yellow bowl.

The mixer slips from her grasp and clatters against the side of the bowl. A ginormous blob of frosting flies off the beaters and lands on the window above the sink with a loud splat. The glob hangs suspended for a second before it starts a slow slide down the glass, leaving a thick smear in its wake.

She switches off the mixer and grabs a dishcloth.

"What? Why on earth not?" she demands as she attacks the mess on the window.

"I'm not entirely sure what the problem is. The reverend just left me a voicemail that he was sorry. He said after double-checking his calendar, he wasn't going to be able to officiate after all. Something about an unavoidable conflict."

She mumbles darkly to herself. Then she twists her neck to look at me over her right shoulder, fixes a bright smile on her face, and chirps, "We'll just see about that."

Despite her cheery demeanor, the glint in her eyes makes me very glad I'm not Reverend Walker.

"Well, it'd be wonderful if you could get him to reconsider because I just don't know how I'm going to find another minister on top of everything else."

"Oh, no. You listen here. There's not gonna be any finding another minister. Generations of Lymans have been baptized, married, and buried by the presiding reverend at the Second Baptist Church. And Roman's not going to be any different, you mark my words."

She's still all fired up, and now she's slapping the frosting on the cake with such force that it's a wonder the entire thing doesn't collapse in on itself.

I fix my attention on my drink to give her a chance to simmer down.

Once she's worked her anger out on the poor cake she turns back to me. "What did you mean, you can't find a new minister on top of everything else? What else is left? I thought you had just about everything planned."

"I did, but my plans are unraveling." I start ticking off disasters on my fingers. Her eyes are getting bigger and bigger.

When I get to the stolen rings, they just about pop out of her head.

"That's a whole mess of trouble," she agrees with a soft sigh.

"It's almost as if the wedding's cursed." I keep my gaze on the table as I say it, but I'm watching her reaction from beneath my eyelashes.

"Pshaw, go on now." She waves her hand at the idea. Then her head swivels toward me. "Did you and Roman have lunch with my mama today?"

I nod.

A knowing expression blooms across her face. "Let me guess. My mother filled your head with stories about the Davis curse."

"She may have mentioned something like that," I allow.

"Mmm-hmm." She steps away from the counter and folds her arms over her chest. "Now, listen here. I love Effie. But there's no arguing the fact that my mother's hanging on to some outdated ideas. And as far as that nonsense about an ancient curse hanging over the family goes, it's pure fantasy. Your wedding's not hexed."

I purse my lips and consider my options. It's clear Denise knows the details about what happened between the families, but from her firm tone and the set of her jaw, it's equally clear she has no plans to share them with me.

I glance around the kitchen looking for inspiration, and a flash of light, like glass glinting in the sun, catches my eye through the window. Outside in the side garden, a small, skinny tree stands framed by the window. It's not much taller than I am, and it's festooned with cobalt blue glass bottles that shimmer in the afternoon light.

I incline my head toward the window. "What a beautiful tree you have out there."

She puffs up at my admiring tone and I can almost see as her thoughts turn from setting me straight to showing off her impressive garden. "Which one do you fancy? The crepe myrtle over in the corner by the perennials? She's a gem, all right."

"Well, I guess it's more of a sculpture than a tree, actually. You know, the one with all the blue glass bottles on it? It's breathtaking."

She tosses her head. "That thing? That's just a spirit tree, honey."

"Pardon?" I play dumb.

"A spirit tree. Folks say if you put those bottles on the tree they'll catch any bad spirits that are about and trap them inside."

"Is that so?"

She narrows her eyes. "But you already know that, don't you, Sage? I see where you're going with this. Just because I indulge in a few rituals and traditions does *not* mean I believe in spirits, hexes, haints, or spells. I'm a good, God-fearing Christian woman."

"Of course you are. But what's the harm in hedging your bets, right?"

"I'm not hedging anything." She fists her hands on her hips. "That tree's decorative; that's all it is."

I may not be a black, middle-aged church lady but I'm not a *complete* pushover. I arch one brow, cock my head, and give her my best 'oh, really?' look.

She stares me down for a long moment, then a hearty laugh bubbles up from her chest. "Okay, fine. I'm hedging my bets."

"So, if you're agnostic about the notion of evil spirits, then surely you leave room for the possibility those spirits could be used against somebody, right?"

"I'm not denying y'all have had a run of bad luck. We'll fix things up lickety-split and get your wedding back on track, but, I'm telling you, you're wasting your time chasing down a curse that doesn't exist."

"Let's forget about the hex for a minute. Is there bad blood between the Lymans and the Davises?"

"You could say that."

"Your mom said the feud began before she was even born. What started it?"

She turns the footed cake plate from side to side, admiring her handiwork for a moment, before she slices two generous slabs of cake and slides them onto purple dessert plates. She plucks two forks out of her silverware drawer and joins me at the table.

I consider demurring, but I figure I need to keep her talking. As long as we're sitting here eating, she'll be inclined to chat. Besides, everybody knows Denise makes a killer cream cheese frosted red velvet cake. I'll regret this during tonight's dance lesson when I'm trying to be light on my feet with a belly full of cake, but I dig my fork into the cake and savor a good-sized bite.

"Well, the details are lost to the fog of time, but the whole mess started over a land dispute."

"A land dispute?"

"Yes, indeed, the Lyman and Davis farms abutted one another and there was some disagreement where the line was. The Lymans called out a surveyor to settle the argument, but Old Man Davis ran him off with a shotgun."

"Good fences make good neighbors," I mumble through a mouthful of the moist, rich cake.

"'Zactly. And it went downhill after that run-in, I imagine. Each family was predisposed to view everything the other did through a lens of suspicion. So what would've been ordinary disagreements between neighbors blew up and turned into this legendary blood feud. So, now all these generations later, the young folks know they hate each other, but they don't even know why."

The cake's amazing, but Auntie Denise isn't really giving me any solid information here. I change tacks. "So, what was the next big blow up, after the property line fight?"

"I suppose that would've been when Effie's Great-Aunt Betsy and Gus Davis fell in love."

"Yeah, I suppose that didn't go over too well."

"Actually, when those two started courting, both families thought it was a great idea."

"They did?" I didn't see that coming.

"Sure. Combined, their land holdings would've been the most acreage owned by Gullahs on the island, maybe anywhere. Mind you, this was in the late eighteen hundreds. Not so long after the Civil War. A union between the Davises and the Lymans could've given both families a real foothold."

"Could've? But didn't? What happened?"

"Betsy fell hard for Gus. But I guess his interest in her was more pragmatic. Or he had a wandering eye. Either way, he was stepping out with another local girl called Ginia. And she found herself in the family way. Old Gus was the daddy."

I shake my head and go for another forkful of cake. To my surprise, I've eaten the entire piece while Denise was talking. I lick the frosting off my fork and return my focus on the story.

"That must've caused a scandal, right?"

"No doubt. But as the story goes, Betsy didn't care. She wanted to be with Gus, and both families pushed hard to make it happen. Gus still wanted to marry her, too. But Ginia's folks put their foot down, and Ginia and Gus were married. Betsy was brokenhearted."

"Did she ever marry?"

"No. She never had another romantic entanglement, as far as I know. She was what folks used to call a spinster, which I think is a hateful word. I prefer single by choice."

We're silent for a moment, both thinking about poor Betsy.

"Betsy and Gus's story is sad, but it doesn't explain why the Davis Family would harbor ill will toward the Lymans," I point out.

"True. But, see, after Ginia ruined the plans to build a land empire, the Davises didn't exactly embrace their new daughter-in-law. And then, Ginia lost the baby. She got it in her head that Betsy had caused the miscarriage."

"What? How?"

Denise shrugged. "I don't know. Probably thought she spelled her. But she went on to have two sons. They grew up with Ginia whispering in their ears about how their daddy's family didn't love them because of the Lymans. That younger boy, he's the farmer who my mom thinks cursed her with scarlet fever."

"So, Ginia and Gus's son is the conjurer?"

"That's what folks say. I don't put any stock in it, myself. And, of course, he's dead now."

She stands and clears the cake plates from the table. My eyes are drawn to the spirit tree outside the window for a long moment.

I turn back to Aunt Denise. "Did he have children, the farmer who Granny Effie had her run-in with?"

"Mmm-hmm. They say he taught them everything he knew about hoodoo. They went on to be very successful, the Davises did. Meanwhile …."

"Meanwhile?"

"You know Effie was married just long enough to have me and Roman's mama, right? Our no-good dad divorced her and ran off to make his fortune out west."

"Roman mentioned it."

"Effie was so het up, she dropped his surname and changed our names back to Lyman, too. And, of course, you know all about what happened between Chip Moore and Trina."

"They never married."

"Mmm-hmm."

"What about you? Why didn't you ever get married?" It's a forward question, but I need to ask it.

She turns away from the sink to face me. "People'll tell you it's the Lyman curse. But the truth is, I haven't met the right person.

It's as simple as that. I sort of think I'd be a nun if we were Catholics." She smiles kindly.

I can see it. I nod. "But, it's true that ever since Betsy's broken engagement with Gus Davis, the Lymans have been unlucky in love. I mean, right?"

"I suppose."

"Who are the remaining Davises? Would any of them have a reason to want me and Roman not to marry?"

She shakes her head but doesn't say anything.

I wait a few seconds. When it's clear she's not going to answer, I stand and kiss her on the cheek.

"Roman and I have a ballroom dancing lesson tonight over in Hilton Head, so I have to get going. Thanks for the cake."

She pats my hand. "Hang on, sugar, I've got something for you."

She flings open the door to the spice cabinet and rummages around in its depths. From the very back, she produces a little sachet of dried herbs and flowers and presses it into my hands.

"You put this in your unmentionables drawer and your luck will turn around." I give the packet a cautious sniff. It has an earthy, musky scent—woodsy, but pleasant.

"Thank you. But what is it?"

"Just a binding love spell a root woman gave me. I haven't had a need for it, but you do."

I tuck the small bag into my purse and wink at her. "Not that you put any stock in magic, right?"

She smiles. "That's right. I don't."

She pulls me in for a goodbye hug. Then she walks me outside, where she stands on the porch and waves goodbye as I back out of the driveway.

When I pull into the street and put the car in drive, I turn my head for one final look at the spirit tree. Brilliant blue light floods my field of vision until I blink.

CHAPTER 5

Thyme

*H*alfway through the first act of "The Merman's Invention," I realize my mind's been fully occupied with worry about Sage. I mean, I can't even say it's wandered. At no point, have I paid the slightest bit of attention to the action unfolding on the stage. (Stage being a relative term, because we're squeezed into the basement of a bookstore and there's no elevated platform where the actors are doing their thing. Maybe I should add another off to the off-off-off.)

I glance at Victor, who's also ignoring the play. He's watching me. Faint worry lines run down his forehead toward his nose as he eyes me.

I raise my index finger to his brow and trace the lines. "What's wrong?" I mouth.

He glances away for a moment, scans the thin program, and then presses his mouth against my ear.

"Let's get out of here."

His warm breath tickles my skin and sends a shiver running down my spine.

I wrinkle my face into a question—*Are you sure?* He nods and jerks his head toward the exit.

We make some noise as we climb over the other theatergoers, mainly because the seats are a hodgepodge of wooden pallets that probably once held books and magazines. They're lighter than they look, and more than one patron is knocked off balance while shifting to let us squeeze by. An actor wearing a gas mask pauses mid-sentence as wood thumps against the hard, bare floor and I pretend not to notice the glares and grumbles as we rush between the rows and out into the small hallway.

Slightly out of breath and giddy, I grab for Victor's hand. "Are you positive you want to leave?"

"If you'd been watching the play, which I don't recommend, you'd know Lynn's character was killed off in the third scene. So she's probably not going to be too miffed about us leaving."

"Oh, I missed that."

"No, really?" he deadpans, and I giggle.

"I'm a little distracted," I admit. "How'd she die?"

"Something to do with the aurora borealis. It wasn't clear."

"What? How much did I miss?"

He inhales, as if he's about to launch into an explanation, then shakes his head. "It doesn't matter. Come on, let's go grab a drink. You can tell me what's going on with you. Because something's on your mind, that much is clear."

By unspoken agreement, we end up at Duke's, right around the corner from my apartment. After we settle into our favorite booth, way in the back corner of the dimly lit bar, Petra materializes and plunks a glass of water and a drink in front of each of us.

"What's this?" I sniff the amber liquid.

"That's a new Scotch. Colin's thinking about carrying it. He had the distributor leave some bottles, told him he'd see what his regulars thought about it. It's on the house. Just let me know what you think." She jabs a finger at Victor's glass. "His is a Dark and Stormy, also on the house because I feel like it."

"Salut," Victor says, tilting his glass toward her.

"Thanks, Petra."

She grins, tosses her bright pink hair, and hurries back to the unattended bar. I clink my glass against Victor's and sip the Scotch. A hint of sweet smoke rolls over my tongue as I swallow.

"It's smooth."

He takes a drink, rests his glass on the table, and slants a look at me. "So, what's going on with you?"

"It's nothing, really. I got these weird texts from Sage today while I was in class."

"Weird in what way?"

"In that she said her wedding's cursed."

He tilts his head to the side. "You think she's having second thoughts about marrying Roman?"

I take another drink before answering. "No, nothing like that. She thinks someone put an actual curse, like a jinx, on the wedding itself."

"Why?"

"I don't know. Because stuff's going wrong. Her florist flaked out on her. And the minister canceled. Something about not being able to find a band. Nothing super sinister. But, she's freaking out and decided it's all because of a curse."

He pushes out his lower lip and nods a couple times, clearly considering this possibility.

"So, like voodoo?"

I blink. "Um ... I'm not sure? Sage says Roman's family has Gullah roots. Would that be—?"

"Hoodoo," he supplies.

"Hoodoo?"

"Without getting too detailed about it, voodoo is a religion. Well, technically, there are lots of ... think of them as denominations ... that make up voodoo. In Brazil, the biggest voodoo sect is called *Candomblé.* But hoodoo isn't a religion; it's folk magic. It has roots in West Africa and is practiced mainly in the South-eastern U.S."

I narrow my eyes. "And you know so much about hoodoo because …?"

"I did a piece a few years back about practitioners of various magic systems in the boroughs."

Victor's a reporter, true. But most of his stories are, um, a little bit boring. It's not his fault; he's currently covering the business and finance beat. I cock an eyebrow. "Really?"

"Really. I'm no expert, but it's not outside the realm of possibility that someone's hexed your sister."

He takes a casual sip of his drink and I sputter. "You believe in magic?"

He answers with a one-shouldered shrug.

"Do you?" I press him.

"I don't know. I know the people I interviewed, the people who practice it, can point to specific instances of casting spells and seeing their desired result happen. Or whatever. Maybe it's self-fulfilling, right? You cast a spell to get a job, for example, and that gives you confidence, so you crush the interview. Or you mix up a love potion, so you're primed to look for romance, and you meet your soul mate the next day. Hell, Thyme, I don't know. Isn't the more interesting question *why* someone would hex Sage and Roman, not *whether* someone did?"

I bob my head from side to side and weigh the question. "Yeah, you're right. I'd like to know why … and who."

"Why and who. That sounds like a job for an intrepid reporter." He raises his glass and grins. There's a familiar glint in his eye. "Mind if I tag along to South Carolina for your spa weekend?"

"You can run around with Roman looking for evil spirits," I tell him. "But you're not horning in on my mani-pedi time with the girls."

"Deal."

CHAPTER 6

Rosemary

I'm scrolling through the latest batch of new home listings the realtor emailed me when Dave pokes his head into the tiny bedroom.

"You busy?"

I glance up. He's got a mug of chai tea in each hand, and the spicy scent wafts across the room.

"Not too busy for you." I power down the laptop and close the lid.

Dave works homicide, and the burnout rate is astounding. Just in the short time we've been together the department's lost three officers. Dave's partner, a terrifying woman named Sullivan (I assume she has a first name, too, but I'll be darned if I know it), spearheaded a program to teach the squad healthier coping techniques.

Instead of washing away the grime and grit of the day with a tall, cold one, they reach for a mug of herbal tea. Instead of racing motorcycles on their days off, they take a yoga class together. Hey, whatever works for them. And, don't forget, this *is* LA.

I set the laptop aside and pat the bed beside me. Mona Lisa opens one eye as Dave's weight shifts her ever so slightly to the left.

"See our dream home in those listings?" he asks as he hands me a mug.

I sip the froth and shake my head. "Not unless our budget's increased, by a lot, without my knowing it."

"Nope. But I'll buy a lottery ticket tomorrow. Problem solved." He rests a hand on the dog's head and gives her a couple good *scritches.* "Do you think Deb could watch our girl this weekend?"

"Sure."

I know without asking that she'd love to. One, Deb is an angel. I mean, if I believed angels walk among us, she'd be the likeliest candidate. And two, she adores Mona Lisa.

"Are you going somewhere while I'm out visiting my sisters?"

"I have some personal time saved up that I need to use before the end of the month. I thought I might invite myself along."

"To Hilton Head? For a girls' spa weekend?"

He shoots me a look. "More like a golf weekend. Roman's been after me to come out and play Chip's home course with him. And I figure he'll be bored because you and Thyme will be monopolizing Sage's time."

"Hmm." I sip my tea.

"Hmm, what?"

"I didn't know you were such a golf fan."

"I swing the clubs now and then."

Not in the three years since I've known you, I think. But I don't say anything; I just eye him over the rim of my raised mug.

He crumbles like a vegan coconut flour and maple syrup cookie.

"Besides, I got a call from Roman. He wants me to help him out with something."

"Help him out with what?"

"Something to do with the wedding." His tone is evasive and he's concentrating on Mona Lisa like he's performing brain surgery on her instead on petting her.

I give him a suspicious look. "Are you talking about a bachelor party?"

"No, but now that you mention it—"

"Don't change the subject. What does he want help with?"

Dave takes a swig of chai and places the mug on the dresser. "Someone broke into his car and stole the wedding rings this afternoon. The local PD doesn't seem to be taking the theft very seriously. I'm just going to help him poke around, check some pawn shops or what have you, and maybe prod the police out there to do some investigating of their own."

I only realize my hands are shaking when hot liquid sloshes over the side of my mug and hits my wrist. I suck in a breath and rest my mug next to his.

"When did this happen—the theft?"

"A few hours ago."

I frown. *After* I spoke to Roman.

I haven't heard anything from Sage since—not a peep about stolen wedding rings. I also haven't heard from Thyme, for that matter. And she definitely would've called if Sage told her about it.

So, Sage is keeping this to herself. It's got to be because she thinks this is all due to her dumb curse.

"Rosie?"

"Hmm?"

"Do you mind if I come along?"

"No, of course not. You're a sweetheart to help Roman. But I'm on to you, detective."

"Oh, yeah? What's that supposed to mean?"

"I know you're a southern boy at heart. This is all a big ruse to get some pecan pie or something, isn't it?"

Dave's family moved around, and he's spent time all over the country, but if you ask him, he'll tell you he's from Georgia.

"Peach. Peach, Rosemary. Otherwise, guilty as charged."

I plant a kiss on his lips as I reach across him for my phone. "Noted."

"So you'll call Deb and work out the details?"

"Sure. Right after I call Sage about the curse."

"The what?"

I shake my head. "It's a long story. I'll tell you all about it later. But the gist is Roman's grandmother has Sage convinced their wedding's been cursed."

He quirks an eyebrow. "Cursed?"

I laugh uncertainly. "It's silly."

Isn't it?

CHAPTER 7

Sage

*A*mazingly, our ballroom dancing lesson goes off without a hitch (other than some stomped-on toes). No fire burns down the studio; our instructor Lucille doesn't fall and hit her head, triggering a bout of amnesia; no swarm of locusts descends upon the island.

After this minor miracle, Roman and I get in our separate cars and he follows me home. As I drive through the quiet neighborhood, with the ocean shining off to my right and the moon rising bright in the evening sky, I'm cautiously optimistic that my luck will turn around.

It's one thing to get caught up believing in spells and spirits out on St. Helena Island, where the Lymans live. The dense vegetation, weathered antebellum architecture, and the creole patois of the long-time residents combine to give off an undeniable Southern gothic vibe.

In contrast, Hilton Head Island's vibe screams new South money and all the security and safety that suggests. Especially Muffy and Chip's exclusive neighborhood. It's about an hour away from where Roman grew up and the Lymans still live, but it may as well be on another planet.

The deliberately quaint and charming beach cottages that line the Moores' road are generously spaced, painted adorable colors, and go for mid-to-high seven figures, easy, if they ever hit the market, which they don't because rich people apparently buy and sell their homes through private sale by casually mentioning over appetizers at dinner that they're thinking about moving and watching their friends scramble for their checkbooks.

The point is, I highly doubt any evil spirits haunt Hilton Head Island. Haunting's undoubtedly against a town ordinance—and probably the homeowners' associations' rules, too.

I giggle at the thought of Chadsworth Connor, the HOA President, writing up a citation for a conjurer with a nonconforming cauldron in his barn—or better yet, a spirit that lacks the proper permits. The day's absurdity finally sinks in, and my mood lightens. I'm humming to myself by the time I turn into the Moores' driveway and drive back to the guest cottage I call home.

After I park, I stand by my car waiting for Roman to pull in behind me. I take a big, deep breath and fill my lungs with warm night air. It's heavy with the tang of the sea and the redolent perfume of Muffy's prized magnolias, which are blooming like crazy. The sky is clear and stars are winking down at me. A light breeze ruffles my hair and plays at my ankles.

I sear the perfect moment into my mind and a quiet flame of hope sparks to life deep in my chest.

I can still pull off my wedding, dammit. And I will. I just need to focus.

As I stand there, pumping myself up for battle, Roman's car crunches along the gravel and comes to a stop in front of me, and Chip Moore pokes his head out the kitchen window and hollers for us to come in for a nightcap.

I stifle a groan.

The situation is sort of weird. I work for Chip and Muffy,

taking care of their truly adorable kids, Skylar and Dylan, and I live in their guest cottage.

Roman also works for Chip. He's Chip's caddy, and, apparently, when you're a professional golfer like Chip, your caddy's part-employee, part-coach, part-friend, and part-right-hand man. In Chip's case, his caddy is also his son.

Unbeknownst to either Roman or Chip when they started working together, Roman is the product of a brief, but intense, love affair between Chip and a local girl while he was in college.

That local girl, Roman's mom, never told a soul who her baby's father was (including said baby), with one exception: she confided in her sister Denise.

Remember what I said about Auntie Denise? Right, she's a force of nature. She managed to meet Muffy through some ladies auxiliary group and casually mentioned her nephew, a talented golfer with loads of natural talent, was looking for work as a caddy.

And the rest, as they say, is history.

Roman's parentage came to light just two years ago, under what can only be described as challenging circumstances.

It's a long story but the short version is this: Some creep figured out that Roman was Chip's son and blackmailed Chip. The creep was murdered (with Chip's eight iron), and Chip was the number one suspect. Chip, however, thought Roman had found out about the blackmail and killed the guy, so was about to take the fall to protect the son he never knew he had. It was a real mess.

Muffy and I cleaned it up as best we could. I identified the real killer, rescued Roman, and we fell in love. And everyone lived happily ever after.

Sorta.

Muffy's been amazing. She opened her heart to Roman without hesitation and went to work making sure he and her kids have a strong relationship.

Chip's been awkward. He tries really hard, but he fluctuates between treating Roman like an employee and being overbearingly fatherly.

Roman is also kind of weird about the whole situation. He's grateful he knows who his dad is now and has this chance to build a connection with him. But sometimes he gets moody and distant when he thinks about all the years he and his mom spent struggling to make ends meet with no dad in sight. And all the while, Chip was living one island away in his perfect house, with his lovely wife and delightful children, and all the perks that come from being on the PGA tour.

Oh, and, Roman's mom is African-American, a Gullah woman from the Lowcountry, while Chip and Muffy are as white as their names sound. And they're local celebrities, members of the golf club, and scions of island society.

As you might imagine, there's a lot of interpersonal stuff swirling around. *A lot.* I've mainly stayed out of it, but planning the wedding has inevitably stirred the pot.

So, while a nightcap with the Moores should sound like a pleasant ritual to wind down the evening, what it's going to be is a minefield, laced with bombs just waiting to explode if we hit on the wrong topic of conversation.

I'm about to beg off, but Roman's already halfway across the lawn. So I square my shoulders and set off behind him. He stops at the porch to wait for me and gives my hand a squeeze.

At first I think he's reassuring me. After a second, I realize he's looking for comfort. So I squeeze back harder.

As we hustle through the kitchen door behind Chip, I catch a glimpse of gleaming braided hair, piled high in a complicated bun on its owner's head. The Moores have company.

Muffy looks up as we enter the alcove off the kitchen. She's sitting in one of the white corduroy chairs that flank the stone fireplace. That pair of white fabric-covered chairs, by the way, came from the most expensive home furnishings store in the Carolinas and is the absolute bane of my existence.

Here's a nanny pro tip: You don't buy white furniture when anyone who lives in your house is in the finger painting and popsicles phase of life. If you truly need the adrenaline rush of living dangerously, take up skydiving or something. But do *not* get a white fabric living room suite, for the love of all that's holy.

At the moment, however, the chair opposite Muffy is occupied by someone who's unlikely to wipe her nose on its arm or curl her shod feet up under her, leaving dirt streaks along the seat.

Hunter Alysse Redforth looks up at us from behind several coats of mascara that, I'll admit, make her bright eyes pop. Her dark, flawless skin glitters, thanks to a subtle illuminating palette that must've been applied with a practiced, steady hand. She smiles widely.

"Hi, Muffy. Miss Redforth."

Muffy gives me an affectionate look and picks up her highball glass. "Why don't the ladies retire to the front room where it's more comfortable, while the gentlemen mix up some fresh drinks?"

Chip crosses the room to fetch the glasses and drops a kiss on the crown of his wife's head.

"Come on, son," he says to Roman. "I'll play bartender and you can catch me up on the stolen rings."

Roman's eyes meet mine and flash good luck. Then he turns toward Chip and the kitchen, "Yes, sir."

"Roman, we're not on the course. Call me Chip. Or Dad."

I wince at the awkwardness in Chip's delivery and catch the teensiest shadow cross Muffy's face as she watches father and son leave the room. Chip's really trying to build a relationship with Roman. But, Lord, he's bad at it.

I notice Hunter watching them, too. Her lively eyes dance with curiosity. I'm sure the high-society gossip beast is hungry for stories about how Chip Moore's dealing with his illegitimate son's upcoming wedding to the household help—and a Yankee, no less.

As I trail Muffy and Hunter into the front room, where there's seating for a crowd, I breathe in through my nose and exhale slowly through my mouth and promise myself not to give Hunter any gossip fodder tonight.

After we get ourselves settled on the couches, Muffy turns to me with a warm smile.

"How was your day off?"

I scan my brain, trying to come up with an answer that's both truthful and unlikely to lead to more questions.

"Productive."

I say it in an upbeat tone, so Muffy can imagine me ticking items off my wedding to-do list while birds flutter around my shoulders like I'm Snow White. And while my day wasn't productive in the sense of actually accomplishing anything, I did learn the reason I'm not making any progress is because I'm under a spell or a jinx or whatever. Isn't knowing your enemy half the battle?

"That's nice," Muffy murmurs. But she's giving me a sidelong look that says she suspects I'm not being entirely truthful.

Hunter pipes up, "Now what's this I hear about stolen rings?"

"Oh, it was the strangest thing. Someone broke into Roman's car while he was at the club and took our wedding rings from his glove box. Can you imagine, at the club?"

I figure if I keep the focus on the location of the theft, Hunter won't want to spread the news around the island. She's in charge of event planning at the club. It would be bad for business if word got around that the parking lot was a hotbed of criminal activity.

Muffy makes a small, sad sound. "I'm sure the police will find your rings before the wedding," she soothes.

"I'm sure they will," I agree.

Just as I'm wondering if Roman and Chip had to go pick the lime for my drink from the tree or what, I hear footsteps.

A moment later, the men appear with a tray full of drinks that they pass around. I take a slow sip of my gin and tonic and pat the sofa beside me.

Roman smiles but cuts his eyes toward Chip. "Uh, we were going to go into the den. Chip wants to show me a new swing-correcting app he has on his tablet."

"That sounds like work, Chip," Muffy observes,

"No, ma'am," Chip assures her, "I'm just showing off my new toy to someone who'll appreciate it."

Chip and Roman leave, trailing laughter in their wake.

Hunter turns to me. "Well, aren't y'all going to have to postpone your wedding, anyway?"

I choke on my cocktail. "Pardon?" I sputter.

"I just mean, between the rings and Jessalyn …"

"Jessalyn?" Muffy crinkles her forehead in confusion.

"Jessalyn James. She owns a dress shop on St. Helena Island. She's doing the alterations for my wedding gown," I explain.

"Was doing the alterations." Hunter corrects me in a gentle voice.

I shake my head. "I'm not sure what you've heard, Miss Redforth, but Jessalyn's shop was closed today because of a family emergency. That's all."

"Hmm. Actually, Sage, Jessalyn's bank foreclosed on her loan yesterday and, the way I heard it, all the dresses in the shop are collateral. So … you don't have a wedding gown anymore."

"That can't be right. I've already paid for everything except the final alterations. I mean, even if Jessalyn's out of business, I can get my dress back. Can't I?" My mind is reeling.

Hunter and Muffy exchange a look. Neither of them wants to say it, but I worked as a forensic accountant for a while before I moved into the attachment parenting consulting business (that's what wealthy stay-at-home moms call babysitting around here).

I'll probably get my dress back … someday, after all the financial transactions are unwound and the secured creditors get paid.

But Hunter's right. It's not going to be anytime soon.

I take a long swig of my drink. This is just great.

"How'd you hear about a dress shop on St. Helena's closing?" Muffy asks her friend.

I perk up a little because I'd like to know the answer, too.

Hunter laughs. It's a delicate, soft noise, the most polite, lady-like laugh imaginable.

"Oh, sugar, I'm a wedding planner, remember? I make it my business to know everything and everyone in the wedding industry space."

"But, you don't work on St. Helena, do you?"

"Gracious, no. My brides come to me to help them create the perfect Hilton Head Island wedding. That's what I'm known for."

That's what I thought. So, I find it unlikely any of Hunter's brides were using Jessalyn for their gowns.

She senses the question. "I have a few girls who considered having Jessalyn do their bridesmaids' dresses. She's a talented sewist. And, for brides on a budget—" she pauses here to wrinkle her nose ever-so-slightly, so slightly that I wonder if I've imagined the movement—"she's a wonderful option. Or at least she was. But I'd heard rumblings months ago that she was in financial trouble, so I've been steering my girls away from her since last summer. None of my brides are caught up in her drama."

She and Muffy fix me with twin pitying looks.

I drain my glass, rest it on the tray, and lean toward Hunter. "I don't suppose you've heard anything about Nolan's Floral?"

This time the nose wrinkle is unmistakable. "Only that they're unprofessional and disorganized. I generally recommend my brides work with Coastal Blooms. But I have used Nolan's to do table arrangements for meetings at the club from time to time. They do fine work, but more than once they've lost my paperwork or mixed up my order with someone else's. Last year, for the Thanksgiving luncheon, they delivered chrysanthemums instead of the Asiatic lilies and hypericum berries I ordered. Can you imagine?"

Unfortunately, I can.

Muffy gives me a close look. "Sage, do you need some help with the wedding? I've told you, I'd love to give you a hand."

She has told me this, multiple times. And, truth be told, I'd love to take her up on the offer. My own mother can't be much help from behind bars; and realistically, wedding planning isn't really MJ Field's thing.

But Muffy's married to Roman's dad. And Roman's mom is already feeling frustrated and helpless because she can't help us financially with the wedding. So, Roman and I have agreed to steer very clear of any involvement by Chip and Muffy. Roman even declined Chip's offer to foot the bill for the rehearsal dinner.

I mean, Skylar is going to be my flower girl; and Dylan's the ring bearer, but the adult Moores have been relegated to guest status only. And hopefully the kind of guests who don't draw too much attention.

"It's so sweet of you to offer," I tell Muffy, hoping she can sense my sincerity. "But I really do have everything under control."

Muffy smiles, but I see the faintest tightening of her mouth. My chest squeezes. I hate to make her unhappy, but I can't see a way to involve her without hurting Roman's mom.

Hunter jumps in again. "You know, Sage, I'd be delighted to plan your wedding for you—"

"I can't afford you." I waste no time cutting her off.

There's no need to be coy about the fact that I'm, as she would say, a bride with a budget. I spare a moment to wonder about the brides *without* budgets, but she's shaking her head and waving her hands.

"No, no. I'd love to do it gratis. Free," she clarifies in English, just in case I didn't catch the Spanish.

Muffy's eyes go wide and she stares at her friend. "You'd do that?"

I can't imagine what Hunter charges to coordinate a wedding, but judging by Muffy's expression, she has some idea, and the number isn't a small one.

Is my crummy luck actually turning around? Has the curse been lifted?

"Well, sure. For Chip Moore's son and future daughter-in-law? I'd be honored."

This sentiment triggers a cascade of emotions, the primary one being that I've not really considered what marrying Roman will mean for my relationship with the Moores. If Chip's going to be my father-in-law, that makes Muffy, my boss, my step-mother-in-law. And Dylan and Skylar, the children I'm paid to care for, will be my brother-in-law and sister-in-law.

My head is spinning woozily, and I don't think it's from the gin.

Muffy and Hunter are both looking at me expectantly, so I shake off the family tree musings and focus on them.

"Sage?" Muffy prompts. "Hunter's offer is very generous. She's been on the Coastal Carolina African-American Women to Watch list for the past three years."

Hunter lowers her eye, bats her lashes, and smiles modestly.

"I'm … wow, that's so kind of you, Miss Redforth."

"Please. If we're going to work together, you need to get used to calling me Hunter."

She raises her glass in my direction.

I'm still trying to find the words to thank her when she drops her bombshell. "Of course, the wedding can't be on St. Helena. It'll be here."

~

I TOSS and turn for a while, listening to Roman's slow, rhythmic breathing. Around two in the morning, I admit defeat and slip out of bed, careful not to wake him.

I ease open the door to the balcony and scoop up a soft fleece blanket from the sofa. It trails behind me like a cape. I curl up in an Adirondack chair and stare out into the dark backyard, not really seeing it.

Hunter's offer to plan the wedding is a problem. Even though she swears on a stack of Junior League membership applications she can pull it off on the budget I reluctantly revealed, I don't believe it's possible.

Not in this town, where a cupcake and a fancy coffee set a girl back twenty bucks. No way.

Over on St. Helena Island, in Frogmore, where Roman grew up, my budget's considered tight, but workable. But Hunter insists the wedding has to take place on Hilton Head.

Muffy immediately offered up the club for the reception, and Hunter promised to give her and Chip a generous discount. I had to shut the conversation down before it got away from me.

I can't ask Roman to have his wedding here. It would be a slap in the face to the Lymans. It would be tantamount to choosing the Moores over his mother, aunt, and grandmother.

He won't do that. I won't ask him to.

Which means I'm right back where I was this morning with no band, no flowers, no dress, and no officiant. Actually, I'm worse off. I forgot to add no rings to the list.

None of this matters, I know. As long as I'm married to Roman at the end of the day, that's all that counts. Intellectually, I get it. But emotionally, I want my wedding day to be beautiful and memorable and a fitting start to the great adventure of sharing my life with the man I love.

Not beleaguered and jinxed.

Hot, fat tears escape from my eyes and I swipe them away

with the back of my hand. Right now, what I want, what I really want, is my mom.

MJ isn't the sort of mother who can fix all my problems with Mary Poppins-like magical efficiency. But she's a good listener, and an empathetic one. And she, unlike my sisters and fiancé, will know what to do about a hex.

I draw a shaky breath. Tomorrow's Thursday, well technically, it's already tomorrow. My parents are permitted to call each of their daughters once a week. Thursday's my day.

I'll be able to talk to my mom. It's not the same as having her here, but maybe she'll have some advice.

I pull the blanket up under my chin and rest my head against the back of the chair. Before I realize it, my eyelids flutter closed and I doze off right there on the balcony, wrung out and exhausted from my craptacular day.

CHAPTER 8

Sage

I wake up when the early morning sun shines directly on my face. I shift and stretch, cold and stiff from spending the night in a wooden chair. I wrap my blanket around my shoulders and try to creep back inside noiselessly.

Half-asleep and still blinking from the sunlight, I smash my shin on the corner of the low bookshelves just inside the door. I jerk my leg back reflexively and my calf catches the sharp inner track of the sliding door. The skin slices open cleanly, right through my thin sweatpants, but I hardly notice because my attention's focused on the sharp pain radiating along my shin.

Man, does it hurt. The agony steals my breath for a second or two. When I get it back, I let loose a string of curse words that would make a rapper blush.

Roman bolts through the bedroom door, his hair spiky and wild, naked from the waist up. As he runs, he yanks a t-shirt over his head and covers his chiseled chest.

"What happened?" he demands with the wide-awake, alert look that comes from an adrenaline rush.

"Nothing. I just hit my leg. I'm sorry I woke you up." I gesture toward the front of my left leg, which throbs and tingles.

"You're bleeding."

I glance down. He's right. Blood is trickling down the back of my leg and pooling around my bare foot. I twist my leg to check out the back. A dark red bloom seeps through my sweatpants. I bite back a few more choice words and limp to the small kitchen area before I stain the carpet any worse than I already have.

He takes me by the shoulders and pilots me into the closest chair. Then he wets a dishtowel and kneels on the floor in front of me, where he props my foot on his solid chest, gently rolls my pant leg up to my knee, and turns my leg sideways to inspect the damage.

I lower my head to see for myself, but he's already pressing the damp, warm cloth against my calf.

"What's the prognosis, Dr. Lyman?" I joke through clenched teeth, trying to keep my tone light.

"You've gonna have a nice bruise on your shin, but that calf's the real problem. I think you need stitches."

I close my eyes and huff out a breath. "I don't have time to go to the ER. Not today."

He taps my forehead with a finger. I open my eyes and glare at him.

He's giving me an *are you for real?* look.

"You know that's not how emergencies work, right? Like, you can't schedule them. Being unplanned is pretty much the definition of an emergency."

I catch myself just as I'm about to snap at him. Instead, I burst into tears.

He watches me with a helpless expression while I sob. After a few seconds, he gathers me into his arms. I cry into his t-shirt and he strokes my hair.

After several minutes of this, I pull it together and lift my head.

"Your shirt's all wet. Sorry."

He shrugs and peels it off. "What's going on with you?"

I'm tired, and jumpy, and out of sorts, and my leg is pounding with pain. But, really, none of this is what has me so worked up.

"It's the wedding," I say in a soft voice.

His amber eyes go dark, the inky black swirls in the center of his eyes grow larger. He bites down on his lower lip.

"You ... don't you want to go through with it?"

"What?" I stare at him uncomprehendingly.

He swallows hard. "Do you want to call off the wedding?"

Understanding dawns. "No. What, are you kidding? No." I grab his hand with both of mine. I can feel his pulse jumping under my fingers. "I want to marry you more than anything else in the world, Roman Lyman."

He exhales, and the light returns to his golden eyes. "Good. So, what's the problem?"

I straighten my spine and force the words out. "Our budget is stretched pretty tight. And now it looks like we're gonna lose the deposit on the flowers *and* I'm going to need to get a new dress. Plus we might have to buy another set of rings. We don't have that extra money laying around. We might need to ... postpone it."

"No." He responds instantly. "We're not delaying the wedding. We'll figure something out."

His fierce certainty is heartening, but I spent most of the night trying to figure something out and failing. So, I'm pretty interested in hearing the specifics.

"Such as?"

He lifts both shoulders. "I guess I could take Chip up on his offer to help out."

He says it as if it's no big deal, but his face is screwed up something awful. He looks just like Dylan when Muffy gets on one of her fish oil kicks and tries to sneak some into the kids' diet via chocolate pudding.

"Or …"

"Or?"

"We could move the wedding here."

"Here? You mean have it in your cottage?" He swivels his head around as if he's calculating the area. "I think it's kind of small, Sage."

"Not in this room, you dope. On the island. Muffy's friend Hunter is a wedding planner. She said—"

"Who?"

I eyeball him hard. Hunter's so gorgeous, she's luminous. Really. She seems to attract all the light in the room, whatever room she's in. The idea that Roman somehow managed not to notice the beautiful woman sitting in Muffy and Chip's living room strains credulity.

I mean, I get it, he loves me. But I love him, and I'm straight, and I noticed her.

"The woman who was sitting next to Muffy last night? You know, she looked like a model? Or an African princess, maybe?"

But he's blinking at me as if I'm speaking a foreign language, so I shrug and move on. I see no reason to die on 'Isn't Hunter Redforth Stunning?' Hill.

"Anyway, she coordinates weddings for a living. She offered to help us out, for free, and said she'd be able to get us some deals. But only if we have the wedding here on Hilton Head Island."

He searches my face. "Is that what you want?"

"No. Yes. Maybe?"

What do I want? I have no idea. I've spent all this time planning a wedding that would make Roman's family happy without offending the Moores, that I haven't stopped to wonder what I want.

"I don't know," I tell him.

"Maybe you should figure that out first. *After* we get your leg fixed up. Come on." He loops my arm around his neck and supports me as we make our slow way to the bedroom for a dry shirt for him and some clean clothes for me.

Then he sweeps me up like it's our wedding night, only he's carrying me across the threshold out of the cottage, not into it. I cling to him as he navigates the stairs. When he deposits me on the ground, I lace my fingers through his and look up at his profile. His chiseled cheekbones and strong chin set off his curly hair and make him look for all the world like a Grecian statue.

"Roman?"

"Hmm?"

"Maybe if we have the wedding here instead of on St. Helena it'll break the curse."

There. I've said it. It's what I've been thinking for the past six hours but I've been afraid to admit it. Now, it's out there. I wait for his reaction.

I see him ball his free hand into a fist and relax it almost instantly. He nods to himself a few times and turns to face me.

"If I can prove to you that there's no curse, can we just move forward with the plans we have?"

I consider this.

"How are you going to prove a negative?"

He snorts. "I have no idea. But if I can satisfy you that there *is* no curse, will you please forget my granny ever mentioned it?"

The way he's phrased it, of course I'll agree to it. "Sure. But if you *can't* convince me that there isn't a curse, can we move the wedding reception to the club and have the ceremony on Hilton Head?"

He locks eyes with me. "You've got it. Now, let's get you to the hospital before you lose any more blood. You look like a ghost."

He bundles me into the passenger seat and I let my head loll back against the headrest. I'm not weak from blood loss, despite his worry. I'm just exhausted.

As he starts the engine, his words echo through my mind, and I drift into a fitful sleep filled with ghosts of Davises and Lymans past. They haunt me all the way to the regional medical center, where I wake up slick with sweat.

CHAPTER 9

Thyme

osemary and I planned our flights to arrive at the Hilton Head Airport within fifteen minutes of each other. The schedule puts us on the island around six-thirty Thursday night. We figure we'll rent a car, grab dinner just the two of us, then check into the hotel. The plan *was* to show up at Sage's cottage bright and early Friday morning and spirit her to the spa, with Muffy's help.

But, as I cool my heels waiting for Rosemary near the baggage claim carousel while Victor checks in at the car rental counter, I switch my cell phone from airplane mode back to normal and it immediately starts blowing up with messages that came in during the four-hour flight from LaGuardia.

A quick scroll reveals that the plans are going to need to change. For one thing, there are four of us now. Rosemary apparently brought her husband along. Not that I can complain about it, seeing as how I've got Victor in tow.

She texted me from her layover in Chicago to let me know

Roman and Sage's wedding rings were stolen last night, and Detective Dave is going to help Roman try to get them back.

I thumb out a reply to let her know Victor can help, too. Dumb, I know, seeing as she's not going to get the message until she's on the ground right outside, but at least everyone will be on the same page when we meet up.

The next message is from Sage. I read it twice, frowning.

Victor materializes near my left shoulder and I glance up.

"What's wrong?"

I try to relax my expression. "Roman took Sage to the hospital today. She sliced open her calf and needed stitches."

He winces. "Ouch."

"Yeah. But she can't drive because she's loopy on muscle relaxers. So Roman drove her to choir practice after work and has to wait to bring her home."

"She was responsible for small children in her condition?"

I shrug. "Muffy has this awesome playroom set up for them. As long as Sage was conscious, they probably entertained themselves. Plus, she was home most of the day."

"Who was?"

"Muffy."

"Remind me again why she has a nanny."

"Attachment parenting consultant," I correct him automatically, scrolling through more texts. "It's so she can leave whenever she needs to. She has social obligations or something. I don't know. Ask someone who's rich."

"So I guess Roman's tied up tonight, huh? That's okay. I'll grab a sandwich and catch the football game while you and Rosemary have dinner."

"Dave's coming, too. So we might as well all have dinner together." I try not to sound disappointed at the development. After all, tomorrow's spa day will be just me and my sisters.

"Cool. What made Dave decide to come?"

"Somebody stole Sage and Roman's wedding rings last night."

He whistles, long and low. "Maybe they *are* hexed."

I don't respond.

My phone dings again. It's Rosemary. The plane's at the gate.

"They're here," I say.

I shoot off a quick text to Roman and Sage:

Me: Do you guys want to meet us (me, Victor, Rosemary, and Dave) for dinner after choir practice?

Roman responds instantly:

Roman: Sage's busy singing, but I'm sure she'd want to see everyone. Didn't know V was joining. Cool! S is pretty beat. How about something easy—like takeout at her place?

Me: Sounds good. 7:30?

Roman: See you then.

I stow the phone and my bag in time to see Rosemary speed walking toward us with Dave at her side. I race to meet her and grab her in a tight hug.

"I missed you!"

"Same." She pulls back and inspects me. "You look good. Tired, though."

I am tired. All that coursework on top of my regular client schedule is kicking my butt. But I just smile. Tonight's not the night to mention I've gone back to school.

I turn to Dave.

"Good to see you."

He releases his grip on the wheeled suitcase he's rolling along and gives me a hug. "You, too, Thyme."

Victor catches up to us, and there's another round of hugs and handshakes before we wander outside to the rental car parking lot.

The early evening air is warm and humid. I shrug out of my sweater and tie it around my waist. Rosemary fishes a hair tie out of her bag and twists her long blonde hair into a loose knot on the top of her head.

While Dave and Victor stroll along talking about work and some big-budget movie I've never heard of, Rosemary loops her arm through mine and slows her pace so we fall behind.

When they're several yards ahead of us, she says in a low voice, "You know this injury is going to make Sage even more convinced she's been cursed, right?"

"Did she say something to you?"

She shakes her head. "No. But Roman texted Dave. Apparently she wants to move the wedding from St. Helena's to Hilton Head and let some fancy pants wedding planner take over."

"A wedding planner? That doesn't sound like Sage."

She bites down and gnaws the lipstick off her bottom lip. "Yeah, I know."

"Stop biting your lip," I order like I'm her mom, not her baby sister. "We'll talk some sense into her tomorrow at the spa."

An uncertain look crosses her face. I wait, knowing she's going to argue with me.

But just then, Dave turns around and hollers for us to stop lollygagging.

Rosemary pastes a smile on her face and says, "Beat you there," before hoisting her bag onto her shoulder and sprinting toward the guys.

I pick up my pace but my mind's still on Sage.

CHAPTER 10

Sage

$\mathcal{J}$ glance around my tiny kitchen and the warm glow of familial love shines out from my chest like a beacon. I realize I'm swaying ever-so-slightly, almost imperceptibly, in my chair and mentally amend the source of my good feeling: it's possible it's Flexeril, not sisterly affection.

Rosemary frowns at Roman and jabs her thumb in my direction. "Just how strong were the drugs they gave her?"

Maybe I'm swaying more than I think? I straighten my spine and give Rosemary a dignified smile.

"Lord have mercy, now she's drooling," Auntie Denise pipes up from the oven she's just preheated.

When she heard about the guys' pizza and beer plan for dinner, I thought her eyes were going to shoot lasers. So she unearthed a casserole and a loaf of frozen bread from the church freezer and insisted on following us back to the cottage to drop it off.

Now, she dusts her hands on an apron I didn't even know I owned. She unties it and hangs it neatly on the hook set in the wall near the pantry. So, *that's* what that hook's for. I've been keeping my purse there.

I snort in secret amusement. Loud, secret amusement, apparently, because five pairs of eyes turn to look at me. I quickly jerk my head and glare at poor Detective Dave as if he were the snorter. But I don't think anyone's fooled.

"Take that out when the timer dings and let it rest for fifteen minutes, you hear?" Aunt Denise instructs Roman.

"Yes, ma'am."

I slide a look in Rosemary's direction. The professional chef is sitting on her hands (literally) and keeping her lip buttoned (figuratively) while Denise bustles around the kitchen.

I have to hand it to my bossy oldest sister; this is evidence of remarkable personal growth. Or even the formidable Rosemary Field Drummond is cowed by Denise Lyman. Either/or.

"Are you sure you won't join us? That seafood casserole looks big enough to feed an army," Thyme says with a smile.

"Not quite an army. I make 'em for the men's guild meetings. It serves a dozen. But you kids go ahead and eat. I need to scoot back over to Frogmore. I'm hosting my book club tonight."

She reaches for her purple boucle jacket and Victor jumps to his feet and takes it from her, holding it so she can slip her arms into it.

"Thank you, dear." She pats his cheek and picks up her pocketbook. "Y'all have a nice night. Roman, could you come help me get something out of my trunk? I have a little get well present for Sage."

I smile at her, giving up any hope of dignity. I'm shooting for non-drooly. "Thanks, Auntie Denise."

She kisses the crown of my head like I'm a child and crooks a finger at Roman, who runs ahead of her to hold the door open. Then he follows her down the stairs.

She's not even all the way down the stairs when Rosemary jumps up and snatches the apron off the hook. She pulls my entire collection of plates (six, white, from the bargain room at IKEA) down from the cabinet. Then she opens my refrigerator and starts rooting around inside.

Dave catches my eye and grins. Yeah, sitting back while Denise was in charge must've been *killing* her.

"What're you looking for?" I ask her. My words sound slurred even to my ears, but maybe nobody will notice.

"A bottle of white wine," she calls over her shoulder.

"But none for you," Thyme adds. I guess she noticed.

"There's wine and beer in the pantry. You'll have to chill it," I tell her.

Outside, a car door—or maybe a trunk—slams shut. Then Denise's engine purrs to life and her tires crunch over the gravel as she pulls out. A minute later, Roman clomps up the stairs and back into the apartment, carrying a tall, skinny cardboard box and wearing a grimace.

He sets the box down on the table in front of me gently but with a distinctly disapproving sigh.

"What is it?" Thyme asks, leaning across the kitchen counter to get a look.

"A piece of junk," Roman informs her as I open the flaps, reach in, and lift out a wire sculpture.

I place it on the table and eye it. It's about two-and-a-half-feet tall with six spindly arms branching off from the center in a seemingly random placement, pointing off in every direction. The sturdy wooden base is in the shape of an X. I twist my lips into a sideways bow as I examine the thing.

"It looks like Charlie Brown's Christmas tree," Dave observes.

Roman cracks a grin. "You're not far off. It is a tree."

It's a tree? I stare at it a while longer, until comprehension pushes through the haze of muscle relaxers fogging my brain and I stand up and peer down into the box.

"Careful," Roman warns as I reach in and start removing the

MELISSA F. MILLER

butcher-paper wrapped objects nestled together at the bottom of the box.

I unwrap the paper from the first one to reveal a smooth, blue glass bottle. I slide the mouth onto one of the tree's branches and push the neck toward the metal trunk.

After I repeat this process five times, I step back to admire the finished product.

The cobalt shines as my kitchen lights glint off the bottles.

Rosemary tilts her head. "It's pretty, in its own way, but ... what is it?"

"It's a spirit tree."

Roman casts a look my way. "It's a folk superstition, that's what it is."

Thyme reaches out and taps a bottle with her fingernail. "So, like a fairy house?"

Roman rolls his eyes so far back into his head that I'm guessing he's examining the inside of his brain.

"Sort of. Only the idea is you want to trap the evil spirits in the bottle, not give them a special home." I twist toward Roman. "Right?"

His only answer is to pull a face and cock one eyebrow like he can't believe this conversation's even taking place.

Victor coughs. "It's commonly called a bottle tree. You'll see them all over the place here and in coastal Georgia. The Gullah people would hang the bottles, originally from the limbs of the crepe myrtle, but nowadays from any tree-like structure, to trap evil haints inside."

"And you know this, why?" Dave asks.

"Did a piece on folk magic a few years ago."

"What's a haint?" Dave wants to know.

"An evil spirit basically."

"So, the spirit goes inside, and then what?" Rosemary chimes in.

"Well, the reason the bottles are usually this shade of blue is because it represents water. And in the Gullah/Geechee tradition, spirits can't cross water. That's also why you'll see so many doors painted a similar shade of blue."

I giggle because Victor sounds so professorial. Thyme shoots me a look and I stop.

He continues, "So the spirit or haint is trapped in the bottle. The trapped spirits moan and howl all through the night—"

"Actually, that noise would be sound waves traveling through a closed-end air column, which is what a bottle is. You know, like when you blow across the mouth of a bottle? It's just the wind," Rosemary interrupts all scientific-like.

"Sure," Victor agrees, affable as ever. "I'm just explaining the story."

"So, the spirit gets trapped in the bottle forever?" our resident homicide detective wants to know.

I'm fascinated to see who seems to be suspending disbelief and who doesn't. The two camps don't break down at all like I expect. So, basically, my oldest sister and my future husband think the idea is ridiculous, while a journalist and a detective seem to be keeping open minds and searching for information. Interesting, isn't it? I realize Thyme's being awfully quiet. Wonder what she's thinking.

Meanwhile Dave's still waiting for an answer to his question. Everyone's looking at Victor, but Roman speaks up.

"In the morning, the sunlight burns up the spirits, leaving the bottles empty and ready to receive another batch of haints. So the story goes." He turns toward me. "I don't think you should put this out in the yard in front of the cottage."

"Why not?"

"It's silly. And Muffy might think it's tacky."

"Muffy's not going to care. It's a thoughtful gift from your Aunt Denise. I'll take all the help I can get turning my luck around. But I'm sure as heck not keeping it inside. I don't want a house full of angry evil spirits."

I stand back up and reach for the tree to carry it outside, but the change in positions makes my head spin. Dizzily, I grab the table's edge with both hands.

Thyme puts a steadying hand on the small of my back and guides me into the chair. My skin feels clammy and my heart is racing.

"Easy, Sage."

Roman relents. "Look, I'll put it outside. Just for tonight. Don't get out of that chair, okay?"

He leans down and brushes my lips with a kiss.

I kiss him back, harder, but wish I had the energy to argue my position: No harm can come from the spirit bottle, and it might just help.

But I'm too tired to express myself, so I lean my head back and watch while he gingerly maneuvers the tree into his arms. Dave gets the door, and Victor helps guide the unwieldy, bottle-laden structure through the doorway.

"We've got ourselves some good guys," Thyme observes.

"Yeah," I say dreamily.

The oven timer dings. Rosemary slides the casserole onto a trivet to cool. Then she comes around to the table and pushes my hair back from my forehead.

"You think you can stay awake long enough to eat?"

"I think so."

She tucks a loose tendril behind my ear. "Listen, I know things have been crappy for you lately. But we're here now, and we're going to help you with the wedding. Promise."

I smile up at her. "Okay."

Thyme elbows her way in between us and loops one arm over my shoulder and the other around Rosemary's waist. "We definitely are. *After* we spend an indulgent day being spoiled at the spa."

I exhale. Maybe everything's going to work out just fine.

CHAPTER 11

Rosemary

*A*fter dinner, Roman convinces Sage to rest with a promise that he'll clean up the kitchen later. Then he heads over to the main house with Victor and Dave. He's going to arrange a golf foursome with Chip to keep them busy while we're at the spa tomorrow. I guess they think they'll find the stolen wedding rings with plenty of time left to play eighteen. *I* think this is a bit ambitious, but nobody asked me.

I turn to Sage, who's stretched out on the couch with her leg elevated.

"Do you get along with Roman's mom?" I ask.

I'm curious what it's like to have your future husband's family hovering around, dropping off casseroles and spirit trees. It's different for me and Thyme. I live clear on the other side of the country from Dave's parents. And Victor's family is in Brazil. But if any of us is equipped to navigate the in-law waters, it's Sage.

She's always been the most social of the three of us. She's a gatherer of people, a hub that connects all these different spokes. And she's as loyal as the day is long. The entire time our parents sailed around the world, from one non-extraditing port to the next, on the run from the law and the three of us were drowning in a sea of their debt, tender-hearted Sage secretly stayed in touch with them.

But, while I've heard her talk about her weekly lunches with Roman's grandmother and singing in the choir with Aunt Denise, she's unusually reserved on the topic of Trina Lyman. I kind of wonder whether Sage's friendship with the Moores isn't a problem for her future mother-in-law, given the history between Ms. Lyman and Chip.

Sage manages a weak smile. Then her normally open expression shutters closed. "She's very busy at work. She manages the biggest department store on St. Helena Island, you know."

I slant a sidelong look at Thyme, who purses her lips and arches one eyebrow but says nothing.

Sage stifles a yawn. Thyme and I exchange looks, and she nods.

"Let's help get you ready for bed. The guys should be back soon, and we'll get out of your hair." She gestures toward Sage's bedroom.

Sage opens her mouth to protest but I cut her off. "She's right. It's been a long, stressful day for you. We'll have all day tomorrow at the spa to catch up."

We stand on either side of Sage and help her to her feet then walk her back to her bedroom with our arms linked as if we're in a three-person version of a potato sack race.

"What if the curse isn't just on the wedding, Rosie? What if my whole relationship with Roman is hexed, forever?" Her voice is drowsy, the words dragged out and soft.

I frown as I formulate a response, but Thyme shakes her head at me and mimes sleeping.

She's right. Sage is three-quarters of the way to dreamland. There's no need to answer.

We get her situated in the bed and Thyme props an extra

pillow under Sage's injured leg. I turn out the lamp on her bedside table, and we tiptoe out into the short hallway to the kitchen. As I pull the door shut behind me, I hear Sage snoring softly.

"She's already asleep," I tell Thyme.

"I'm not surprised. She's had a long day."

"Sounds like she's had a long week."

By unspoken agreement, we rinse the dishes and load the dishwasher. I soak Denise's casserole pan in hot soapy water while Thyme wipes down the counters.

The entire process takes about three minutes. Then we stand in the middle of Sage's quiet cottage and look around.

Thyme gestures to the wine bottle. It's two-thirds empty. "Might as well finish that while we wait for the guys."

I pour a glass for each of us, and we head out to Sage's small balcony with our drinks.

"This curse thing ..." I begin. I let the sentence trail off because I'm not at all sure how to end it.

Thyme sips her drink. After a moment, she says, "Do you hear that?"

I listen. "Hear what?"

She cocks her head toward the garden. "That."

"All I hear is the wind."

"Right, that moaning. It must be the breeze passing over Sage's bottle tree."

"Or the spirits trapped inside," I crack.

Thyme gives me a thoughtful look. She doesn't laugh.

I nearly spew chardonnay all over myself. "Come on, Thyme. Tell me you're not going over to the dark side. There are no evil spirits."

She traces a circle around the base of her glass. "Look, I'm not saying the wedding's cursed." Even though we closed the glass sliding door behind us and Sage is sawing logs two rooms away, she drops her voice to a near whisper. "But something's going on. I mean, all this bad luck can't just be a coincidence."

"So what *are* you saying?"

"I don't know. But I don't see any harm in hanging some bottles from a tree and hoping it helps."

I exhale through my nose. "The harm is Sage is focused on lifting the curse or appeasing the spirits or whatever when she should be spending her time getting her plans back on track."

She puts a hand on my arm. "That's why we're here, remember? Just let her enjoy her spa day tomorrow, and then I promise you can take out a notebook and make one of your soul-crushing to-do lists, okay?"

I try to smother a grin but fail. It's a fair comment, and we both know it. "We're way past handwritten to-do lists. This situation calls for a spreadsheet. But don't worry, I made one on my tablet during the flight today."

"Of course you did." She gives my shoulder a light punch. "And I'm sure it'll save the day. But try to ease up on Sage about the spell. You know how she is."

I nod my agreement and turn my attention back to my wine. That's the problem. I *do* know how Sage is. And she's wired to overlook the real-world situation and obsess about some supernatural hoodoo problem. She's nothing if not Mary Jane Field's daughter.

CHAPTER 12

Thyme

*M*y phone rings while Victor's bringing the bags up from the car. Rosemary and I swapped our room for two adjoining suites because bunking with your sister's one thing. Bunking with your sister and her guy *and* your guy ... that's another kettle of fish. So she's on the other side of a solid wall. But, even so, when Blue Mountain FCP, the minimum security federal prison camp my mom calls home (for at least another six-to-nine–months), scrolls across my phone's display, my immediate thought is *I don't want Rosemary to overhear this conversation.*

Don't be ridiculous, I scold myself before taking a cleansing breath and picking up the call.

"Mom, is everything okay?"

"As okay as it can be when one's wearing an orange jumpsuit, dear."

I manage a nervous laugh. "I just thought something might be wrong with you—or Dad." Dad's just down the road (and on the other side of the barbed wire fence) at the Blue Mountain West, the men's facility. Mom tells people it's like they're at single-sex sleep away camps. But somehow I doubt the wardens get their respective charges together for dances and field days.

"No, no, your father's fine. I just saw him at the backgammon tournament yesterday. We ladies cleaned their clocks."

She chortles, and I revise my assessment of the summer camp analogy.

"Why are you calling tonight, then?" My assigned day for calls from Mom is Monday.

"Well, honey, I'm concerned about Sage. I called her at the appointed time but she didn't pick up. And she hasn't called me back. Lights out is in ten minutes. So I just wanted to check and see if you'd heard from her?"

I can hear the anxious quaver in her voice. Only a mom would be worrying about her grown daughter's safety from within the big house.

"She's okay, Mom."

"You've talked to her then?"

"Um, actually, I saw her. Rosemary and I came to town to help her with some wedding stuff. We got in earlier this evening." Even though, intellectually I know it's not my fault she committed tax evasion and fraud, I feel a twinge of guilt that I'm here and she's not.

"Oh, that's nice of you girls." Her tone sounds wistful, and the guilt twists my gut.

"Have you heard anything about your furlough request?"

"As a matter of fact, we have. As long as your father keeps his nose clean, that nice young man from the IRS, Colin Morgan, has convinced both wardens to approve a social furlough for us. Because we're a flight risk, we'll have to pay to have two corrections officers escort us. But we can come. I was hoping to tell Sage the good news tonight."

"That's great! Wait, has Dad been getting into trouble?" My

mind finally catches up with the part about him keeping his nose clean.

"Not exactly. Not yet. He's taking bets on the board games, though."

"Dad's a prison bookie?"

"He says it gives him something to do, keeps his mind sharp."

"Tell him I'll send him more crossword puzzles and Sudoku books. He has to stop that—Sage needs you two at her wedding." My tone's sharper than I intend.

"What's going on? Why didn't Sage answer her phone?"

She can tell. I don't know how, but she can sense something's wrong.

"Sage banged up her leg this morning—"

"Banged it up how? Can she walk? Is she paralyzed?"

"Mom, calm down," I start talking over her as loudly as I dare. The last thing I want to do is make so much noise that Rosemary comes over to check on me. "She just bruised her shin and sliced up her calf. It was a pretty deep cut, so Roman took her to the hospital to get stitches. I guess she cut a muscle or something because her leg keeps cramping up. But they fixed her up and gave her some muscle relaxants. She's going to be fine. But that's why she didn't answer her phone. She's zonked out."

"How'd she hurt herself?"

"I think she just tripped or something."

"Bad luck," Mom muttered.

"You don't know the half of it."

"What's that mean?"

Crap. Way to go, Thyme. Way to open your gigantic yap.

"Um, nothing."

"Thyme Peppermint Field. What's going on?"

I cringe at the use of my full name. Not because I have a latent childhood memory of knowing I was in trouble when she trotted out my middle name, but because said middle name is Peppermint. I mean, *come on*. There's a reason why Rosemary Vanilla,

Sage Almond, and I didn't ditch our New Agey first names in favor of our middle names. That reason should be fairly obvious.

"It's not a big deal. Sage has been having a run of bad luck lately. Her leg was the proverbial straw."

"What kind of bad luck?"

I hesitate. I really, really, *really* do not want to get into the whole curse thing with my mother. But she's going to eventually find out (like as soon as she talks to Sage). Then she'll be irritated I didn't tell her.

"Listen, we're going to see Sage in the morning. Do you want me to tell her the good news or will they let you call her again tomorrow? She'll be so excited!" This is true. And I need to know if I have to provide her with a full accounting now or if I can put it off.

"I'll ask my unit leader at our morning meeting. I'm pretty sure she'll let me call after breakfast."

Yay.

"Great," I say feebly. "So, before you talk to Sage, you should know that a lot of things have gone wrong recently—just typical planning hiccups and bumps in the road. But, she's got this idea that a conjurer has cursed her wedding."

"Sage crossed a *root man?*"

I hold the phone away from my ear. "Sage didn't cross anyone, Mom. Roman's family has some ancient feud with the neighbors or something. And his grandmother convinced Sage that a descendent of this so-called root man or conjurer or whatever cursed the wedding."

I think that's the story. Or is it the spirit of the long-dead conjurer himself, still pissed off like a hundred years later, who's supposed to have put the hex on the wedding? I realize I never got the details.

"Thyme, I need you to listen to me. This is important, okay?"

"I'm listening."

"Tell Sage to smudge her entire home. She needs to get a bundle of dried white sage and—"

"Mom, she knows how to purify a space by burning sage." We all do. We grew up smudging every room in the resort on a regular schedule.

"Don't interrupt. My time is almost up. She should burn some sweetgrass afterward."

"Okay, I'll tell her."

"Thyme." Her voice is a warning.

"I promise, I'll tell her. But, look, this should make you feel better, Roman's aunt gave her a spirit tree for protection, and I saw some sort of sachet on her bedside table when I was helping her get ready for bed. The Gullah/Geechee have their own rituals, okay? You don't have to worry about this."

"Good, good. Did you say Gullah? I think one of the girls over in Cell Block D is Gullah. I'll ask Charla for some tips during library time."

"Great idea. But, honestly, Mom, the most important thing you can do for Sage is to make sure you and Dad are there at the wedding—and try not to get yourselves abducted in the process." I throw in a reference to Rosemary's wedding, which saw her and my parents held captive in a storage pod.

My attempt at comedy falls flat, though, and my mom sniffs. "Well. Unlike your oldest sister, Sage has actually invited us to her wedding. We won't have to skulk around in the bushes like criminals."

"But you *were* criminals." The words fly out of my mouth and I clamp my hand over my lips as if that's going to help.

"Thyme Peppermint!"

Twice in one call. Yeesh.

"Sorry, Mom. I didn't mean it as a bad thing." Weak, I know. But I don't know what else to say.

"I just hope that you and Victor wait until your father and I are released to tie the knot. I'd really love to help one of my girls plan her wedding. Do you have any idea when he—?"

I suddenly desperately wish we were still talking about Wiccan cleansing rituals. "Victor and I haven't ever talked about marriage, Mom. I'm not in any hurry."

"Hmm. You say that now. But, you know, your eggs are as old as you are. They're not going to stay fresh forever. If you think you might want to have children, you really—"

There's a loud knock on the door. I send up a silent *thank you* to the Universe.

"Mom, there's someone at the door. Gotta go. Love you, 'bye!"

I jab the button to end the call and peer through the peephole. Not surprisingly, it's Victor with the bags. I yank the door open.

"Boy, am I glad to see you." I plant a kiss on his lips as he tosses the bags on the suitcase stand near the door.

"How long was I gone?" he asks in an amused tone.

"Too long."

"I see. You seem to have missed me."

"You don't know the half of it."

He smiles a crooked smile and traces a finger along my collarbone. "Why don't you show me how much you missed me?"

I grin up at him, lace my hands together behind his neck, and lower myself to the bed, pulling his mouth down to meet mine in the process. He stares down at me hungrily while our tongues explore each other's mouths.

All thoughts of evil spirits, meddling mothers, and wedding jinxes evaporate, no doubt vaporized by my rising body temperature. I arch my back, straining toward him and he smiles a lazy smile.

CHAPTER 13

Sage

ou'd think I'd wake up feeling refreshed and ready to take on the world after sleeping for eleven hours. You'd be wrong.

I lie in bed feeling for all the world as if I'd been flattened by a steam roller during the night. My body aches, my mouth is cottony, and my brain is a fuzzball. I stare at my alarm clock and try to figure out what day it is.

Roman's side of the bed is empty. So it's probably a weekday. He sleeps over most nights because my place is bigger and more comfortable than his apartment. (His design aesthetic is apparently 'minimalist bachelor meets 1980s Eastern bloc government drab.' Think lots of metal and institutional gray-green furniture.)

But he likes to get up early and work out at the gym near his place before driving back here and meeting Chip at the club. Or so he says.

I think it's probably more that he feels weird sleeping over at my place seeing as how his boss/dad owns the joint and my boss/his stepmom and my charges/his half-siblings all know when he's here and when he's not.

I get it. As the care provider to two impressionable kids, I don't exactly enjoy the fishbowl aspect of our living arrangement.

Even through my brain fog, this series of thoughts drives home the fact that our current arrangement is … weird. Like dysfunctional reality show weird. Or heavily monetized YouTube channel weird.

Somehow, this meandering train of thought leads me to the realization that it's Friday. It's Friday, and I have the day off because it's Spa Day.

I stretch my arms behind my head and stretch until my fingertips graze the wall. Then I extend my legs toward the end of the bed … and my gentle morning stretch turns into a horror show. Searing pain shoots up my leg like fire. I whimper then gasp for breath like a landed fish. Damn, that hurts.

I lift the sheet and peek underneath to examine my injuries. A deep purple bruise covers my shin from just below my knee almost to my foot. Lovely.

I twist my leg to check out the stitches and break out into a sweat from the pain of moving it. It proves not to be worth the suffering because all I can see is a thick white bandage covering the steri-strips.

I flop back onto the pillow and try to catch my breath. Who'd ever think a stupid cut would hurt so much?

I eye the prescription bottle on my bedside table but decide to pass. I think I'd prefer leg cramps to the spacey, unfocused feeling I had last night.

Speaking of last night, I try to remember how I got into bed and fail spectacularly. Nice.

I reach for the sachet that Denise gave me and turn it in my hands as I consider my day. Nothing bad's going to happen, I tell myself with a confidence I don't feel.

Even if the curse is real, it's directed at the wedding, I reason. Not my entire life. Not my sisters. I clear my mind of worry and ease myself out of bed.

I gingerly test putting weight on my bad leg and shuffle off to the bathroom to get ready for a relaxing, curse-free day with my sisters.

I eat a bowl of oatmeal and manage to get myself down the stairs to wait for my sisters to pick me up. I sit in a lounge chair and watch the butterflies flit through Muffy's garden and chase each other around my bottle tree in a lively game of aerial tag until the rental car turns into the driveway.

Rosemary and Thyme are cheery and raring to go. Thyme hands me a travel mug filled with my favorite chai latte, and we head off to Saltwater & Serenity for our day of restorative self-care.

The spa is spectacular. Soothing colors, sparkling lights, and soft music set the tone. We change into sleek, cloud-like robes and sip cucumber-mint water and herbal tisanes in front of a crackling fire.

Rosemary had the good sense to reserve a private room for us to retire to between treatments, so we can gab and giggle to our hearts' content without worrying about intruding on anyone's zen.

First, we catch up. Rosemary shows us pictures of the houses her realtor sent her and cracks us up with her stories about their mortgage broker, who tried to convince them that a holistic caterer and a homicide detective could totally afford a million-dollar home.

"He said he had clients who were a cat manicurist and a part-time found art poet who were approved for a loan for a four-million-dollar mansion in Santa Monica Canyon," she tells us between fits of laughter.

Then it's time for (human) manicures and pedicures. Shelly,

who does my nails, assures me that feline manicures haven't made their way this far east. Yet.

We reconvene at the fireplace, feet scrubbed, buffed, and lotioned, and fingers and toes polished.

I prop my left leg up on a fluffy pillow and lean back against the arm of the loveseat. Rosemary nabs us some fruit, nuts, and cheese from the snack station, and Thyme declares it's time for mimosas. As if she's been hovering in the hallway, just waiting for her cue, an attendant sweeps into the room balancing a silver tray laden with three champagne flutes, a bottle of bubbly, and a crystal pitcher of orange juice. She places the tray on the low table in front of the fire and proceeds to make our first round of drinks with quick, fluid movements.

She's halfway out of the room before we've finished thanking her.

Rosemary passes out the champagne flutes and raises hers in a toast. "Here's to spa days with sisters. May we not wait until the next wedding for our next one."

"Here, here," Thyme agrees.

I clink my glass against theirs and take a sip of the sweet, effervescent drink.

"Speaking of weddings, you're next," I crack, raising an eyebrow at Thyme.

She rolls her eyes. "You sound like Mom."

I choke on my mimosa. "Oh, no. I just remembered, Mom called me yesterday while I was getting my leg fixed up. I never called her back." My giddiness goes flat like cheap champagne, not the good stuff they serve here.

Thyme pats my arm. "Don't worry. When she didn't hear from you, she called me. I told her what happened. She's going to try to call you this morning after her unit meeting."

Relief floods my body and I exhale. "Thanks. I can't believe I spaced on calling her back."

Rosemary snorts. "I can. You were pretty loopy last night."

After she stops giggling, Thyme adds, "If I tell you something, you have to pretend to be surprised when you talk to Mom. Deal?"

"Deal."

She rests her glass on the tray and leans forward, her eyes bright with excitement. "Mom and Dad will be at your wedding!"

A jolt of joy zips through me. "Really?"

"Really. As long as they manage to stay on good behavior until the wedding, they've been granted a social furlough."

Rosemary claps her hands together and squeaks, "I'm so happy for you!"

It's clear from her face that she means it, which is a relief. I've never been sure she's totally forgiven me for going behind her back to invite our parents to her wedding on the down low—or our parents for making the surreptitious invite necessary in the first place.

"Now this is news worth celebrating. To Mom and Dad," I say as I lift my glass again.

"To Mom and Dad," Thyme says.

"To Inmates Number 628994-087 and 628994-088," Rosemary chimes in.

Okay, maybe she hasn't completely forgiven Mom and Dad. But, it's mostly water under the bridge.

Thyme pauses with her glass halfway to her lips. "Oh, and I promised Mom I'd tell you to smudge the cottage."

Rosemary narrows her eyes. "Why would Mom randomly say something like that?"

"I kind of mentioned the curse."

"You what?"

"Sage is going to tell her when they talk, and you know it. What was I supposed to do? Not saying anything would just delay the inevitable and make Mom think she can't trust me."

My eyes ping-pong between them as they go back and forth,

talking about me as if I'm not in the room. I refill my mimosa glass and watch the action until they remember I'm there.

"Sorry, Sage. Anyway, you know Mom. She just wants you to make sure your space is purified." Thyme smiles at me.

Rosemary's rolling her eyes.

I turn to her. "You know, for all your snark about positive energy, I seem to remember seeing a display of energy crystals on your side table the last time I was out to visit you."

Thyme's mid-gulp when I say this, and she devolves into a full-on choking fit. A flush creeps up Rosemary's neck to her cheeks and she lowers her eyes but doesn't respond.

Just then the door opens and three white-clad spa employees crowd the doorway.

The woman in front says, "Ladies, are you ready for your massages?"

"Yes." Rosemary drains her champagne flute and jumps to her feet.

Thyme shakes her head and helps me into a standing position. "Enjoy your massage," she tells me as she hands me off to my massage therapist, a willowy redhead whose nametag identifies her as Carla.

I wave goodbye to my sisters as they pair off with their massage therapists. Carla leads me down a long hall. The walls are painted a pale blue and the overhead lights glow a soft amber.

"I have to take it slow," I explain, pointing to my leg. "I hurt my leg."

Carla smiles and offers me an arm for support. "We'll avoid that area during your treatment, shall we?"

"Please." I booked a hot stone massage because there's nothing like the feeling of melting into a puddle of pure, blissful relaxation, aided by the warm heat from the stones. But I'm fairly certain that if Carla so much as thinks about touching my left leg, I'll have her in a chokehold before you can say 'ohm.'

She asks me about my sisters, and I prattle on until we reach the treatment room, which is dimly lit by candles and glowing pink Himalayan salt rock lamps. She helps me up onto the massage table, and we arrange a nest of neck bolsters as a support for my injured leg. Then Carla covers me with a thin blanket that's come straight from a warmer, and I wriggle out of the robe and let it slip to the floor. Not the usual way of disrobing before a massage, I realize, but there was no way I could have gotten onto the table without her help. This stupid cut on my leg is a bigger hindrance than I expected it would be.

I silence the whining voice in my head, close my eyes, and prepare to sink into a relaxed state.

Carla moves around the room quietly, almost silently, opening bottles of oil and removing the stones from their warmer with a series of soft clinks as they knock against each other. The only other sound is the faint, piped-in instrumental music with nature sounds in the background.

I exhale deeply.

The next thing I know, I'm waking up, wiping my mouth with the back of my hand. *Great, I'm drooling.*

I lift my head. Carla's standing at a small metal sink in the corner of the room, washing her hands.

"Did I snore?"

She turns to smile at me. "Did you have a restful nap?"

"Evidently."

"Your body must have needed the sleep. You didn't stir once, not even when I repositioned you."

I'm too jelly-like to do much more than smile dazedly at her. She helps me into my robe, reminds me to drink lots of water for the rest of the day, and leads me back to the private lounge.

Thyme and Rosemary are already back in their chairs, working on the pitcher of mimosas. They look the way I feel—glowy and at peace.

"How was your massage?" Rosemary asks as Thyme hands me a glass of water.

"I assume it was divine. I slept through it."

She laughs. "You didn't."

"I did. From start to finish. What about you?"

"Amazing," Rosemary declares. "I had an aromatherapy massage, and I feel much more balanced."

"Yeah. Leave it to our resident skeptic to get her chakras balanced," Thyme observes dryly.

"What did you get?"

"A deep-tissue massage. I really needed it. Lately my clients have been requesting a lot of yoga shred-style classes. That's hard on the body," Thyme explains.

"How's work going, anyway?"

She shrugs. "Work's fine. I'm tired, though. I've started taking classes again. It's kicking my butt."

Rosemary and I both squeal in excitement.

"Are you going to go for your Ph.D.?" she asks at the same time I say, "Will you find a research lab to join?"

Thyme holds up her palm like a crossing guard. "Slow down, and one at a time. I'm not sure what I'm going to do. I'm noodling on the idea of incorporating some evidence-based behavioral psychology into my personal training. It would be more of a coaching situation. Nothing's set in stone."

"I'm so happy you're doing it," I tell her.

I am. I can tell from Rosemary's wide grin that she is, too. We all veered off our original career paths when our parents went on the lam and stuck us with their enormous debt. But, we've paid that off, and now we're slowly realizing we can do something different now.

Rosemary opened her catering business, and now Thyme's gone back to school. I'm proud of them, and my heart's full for them. And only the teensiest part of me wonders what exactly I plan to do with the rest of my life. Muffy doesn't really need me anymore. She knows it, and I know it. The kids are at school half-days now. Next year, Skylar will be gone all day. And the year after that, Dylan will follow.

It'd be pretty hard to be a nanny to no children. Muffy'll help me find another position if I ask her to. I just don't know what I want to do when I grow up.

I realize my sisters are both studying me.

"What?"

"You look lost in thought," Thyme says.

"Sorry. Daydreaming. I'm so excited for you."

She grins. "We have an hour until our lunch reservation and no more appointments until this afternoon. Do you guys want to check out the steam room and whirlpool?"

"Sure."

"Why not? There's a swimming pool, too," Rosemary informs us.

We slip our feet into the soft terrycloth slippers that match our robes and pad out of the room. After putting on our bathing suits in the dressing room, we re-robe and stop by the front desk to ask for directions to the aqua spa.

"Oh, I can show these ladies the way," a familiar honeyed voice drawls.

I turn. "Hunter?"

Hunter Redforth blinks at me. "Why, Sage, what a nice surprise."

The fresh-faced young woman behind the desk looks from Hunter to me and back to Hunter. "Are you sure you don't mind, Ms. Redforth?"

"Not a bit. It's no trouble." She slips her arm through mine and points to a door on our right. "We're going to go through this door and downstairs. Who are your friends, Sage?"

I blush. "Oh, sorry! Hunter, I'd like you to meet my sisters, Rosemary and Thyme. This is Hunter Redforth; she's a friend of Muffy's."

We stand in the foyer and do a round of hellos, nice to meet yous.

"Isn't this just such a nice treat?" Hunter enthuses.

"The spa's lovely," Rosemary agrees.

"And it's serendipitous that I get to meet the bridesmaids before the wedding. I usually like to get to know all the players before the big day. Oh, I assume they're both bridesmaids?" Hunter asks somewhat belatedly.

"They are."

Thyme shoots me a puzzled look, so I explain, "Hunter's a wedding planner. She's offered to help me with the arrangements, maybe."

"Maybe?" Thyme's quizzical expression deepens.

"If I end up having the ceremony and reception here instead of in Frogmore," I elaborate.

"You're not changing venues," Rosemary says in her bossiest big sister voice.

Hunter's right eyebrow quirks up pointedly. "I don't think your sister's going to have a choice. At least with regard to the church. Didn't Muffy tell me Reverend Walker has a conflict?"

"Um, that's right," I answer slowly. I have no memory of mentioning that fact to Muffy, but I must have. I make a mental note to pitch the remaining muscle relaxers in the trash because they've apparently turned me dopey.

"Is there another minister at Second Baptist who's available to officiate?"

"Not that I know of. But I could bring someone in, couldn't I? I mean, I'm not saying I've decided to go forward with the wedding on St. Helena Island. I just … Roman and I are still discussing our options."

I shoot both Hunter and Rosemary looks intended to say 'back off.' In Hunter's case, it's a gentle warning. In Rosemary's case, it's somewhat less gentle. But she's earned it.

"Hmmm. Well, don't talk too long. The closer we get to the

date, the harder it's going to be to make new arrangements, Sage." Hunter's smile is professional and her voice is as liquidy as ever, but her words carry a thin edge of steel.

"I understand. Roman and I will make a decision over the weekend. Why don't you and I plan to talk on Monday?"

"Perfect," she coos as she sweeps open a wide door marked 'Ladies' Water Amenities' and gestures for us to go inside. "Here we are. My recommendation is to start in the plunge pool, then hit the sauna, the whirlpool, and the plunge pool again in that order. Then float around in the saltwater pool to your hearts' content."

"Thanks, Hunter. It was nice to meet you," Thyme says, ever polite.

"You as well. I look forward to working with you girls to make your sister's big day as memorable and stunning as she is."

Rosemary mutters under her breath something that sounds like 'She doesn't lack for confidence, does she?' and I have to agree.

"Bye, Hunter."

When she's halfway through the doorway, she pivots gracefully in place. "Oh, I nearly forgot. Let me show you where the towels are."

"We'll find them, really. It was kind of you to walk us down, but you don't want to be late for your appointment." I gesture toward her spa-issued robe and slippers. She's obviously here for some pampering of her own.

"Don't be silly. They'll wait for me. I come in regularly to try their new offerings, so I can share my thoughts with my brides. Now, just follow me this way." She heads to the back left corner of the room.

I catch Rosemary and Thyme's eyes and raise my shoulders in a small shrug. The three of us trail behind Hunter even though I'm positive we could manage to find the towel service on our own.

"And here we are," she trills when we reach a counter piled high with fluffy petal pink and baby blue towels.

"Thanks again, Hunter."

Just then the towel attendant pops up into view on the other side of the counter.

"Hello, ladies. I was just folding this load of towels. They're fresh from the dryer, still warm." Her rich voice is warm, and she speaks with the familiar Gullah accent I know so well from my time on St. Helena.

"Thank you." I take the towel she proffers, which, as advertised, is warm and smells like springtime.

Thyme and Rosemary reach for towels of their own and thank the woman. She extends a towel toward Hunter, who waves it away.

"No, thanks. I'm on my way back upstairs."

The attendant squints at her. "Allie, my goodness, look at you!"

Hunter's face freezes in a perfectly flat expressionless mask. It's as if she's been stealth Botoxed somehow.

"I'm afraid you have me mixed up with someone else," she says after a slightly-too-long pause.

The older woman purses her lips. "I don't think so. You're Davina and Clovis's girl."

Hunter draws herself up stiffly and speaks in a tone that suggests the woman is stupid beyond measure. "You're confused. My father's name is Jerome Redforth, and I've never seen you before in my life. Now, if you'll excuse me."

She turns on her heel and huffs away. I can almost see the trail of ice she leaves in her wake.

The towel attendant turns away, too, after throwing Hunter's departing back a dark look. She grumbles to herself as she resumes stacking towels.

We take our fresh towels and wander back toward the pool area.

Thyme breaks the silence. "Well that was weird."

"Your pal Hunter sure is touchy about mistaken identity," Rosemary observes.

I ease myself into the cold water of the plunge pool and sit against the wall before answering. "I wonder if it's a class thing? Hunter moves in a certain social circle, which I assume doesn't include towel attendants."

Thyme sits on the edge of the pool and dips her ankles into the water, swinging them back and forth. She wrinkles her nose. "I like her less and less by the second."

Rosemary, as usual, has the last word. "It doesn't matter. We're going to show Sage that there's no curse and her wedding'll go forward in Frogmore, as planned."

After that pronouncement, she bounces on her toes and jumps into the pool with a tremendous splash that sends cold water all over Thyme and me.

CHAPTER 14

Rosemary

 $\mathcal{A}$ fter lunch, we return to the lounge room and a fresh pitcher of mimosas. Thyme takes a nap, Sage reads a book, and I fret. A suspicion's been building in my brain, and it's threatening to burst out of my mouth.

I manage to keep my lips firmly closed until the smiling aesthetician comes to escort Sage to her facial appointment. Seeing my chance, I elbow Thyme awake.

"Ow." She glares me and rubs her ribs. "What was that for?"

"It's time for our facials, but I need to talk to you first."

She yawns, stretches, and looks around. "Where's Sage?"

"On her way to get her facial. Wake up and listen to me for a second."

"I'm listening."

"I think Roman's mom is trying to derail the wedding."

I sit back and watch her face for a reaction. She scrubs her hand over her eyes then rubs her forehead.

"What are you talking about?"

"Think about it, Thyme. Trina would know all about the

Lyman curse. She lives on St. Helena Island and has easy access to all the service providers who've been flaking out on Sage. She might even have a spare key to Roman's car. It'd be a piece of cake for her to steal the rings."

Thyme raises her arms over her head and stretches to her left. She repeats the motion on her right side.

"Solid theory, Rosemary. Just one question."

"Yes?"

"What earthly reason would Roman's *mother* have to try to screw up his wedding plans?"

I nod. "Right, motive. I'm glad you asked. She doesn't want to see Roman marry a woman who lives on Hilton Head Island. She might lose him. You saw how Hunter treated that poor woman at the pool. There's a big divide between the two islands."

She makes a soft *hmming* noise and tips her head from side to side. "Sage *did* sort of say she and Trina aren't that close, didn't she?"

"She certainly implied it. It's clear Denise and Roman's grandmother love Sage. But I never hear anything about his mom."

"No, she mainly talks about ..."

"Chip and Muffy," I finish for her. "Which is another reason Trina would be against the wedding. Marrying Sage just solidifies Roman's connection with the Moores and makes his dad and stepmother an even *bigger* part of his life than they already are. If I were Trina Lyman, it would tear me apart to watch the son I raised singlehandedly getting so cozy with the dad he never even knew."

She bobs her head again, more enthusiastically this time. "Maybe. But what do you suggest we do about it?"

The door to the lounge swings open.

"Thyme? Rosemary? Are you ready to get your glows on?"

I flash the aestheticians a quick smile and whisper in Thyme's ear. "You and I are going to go to Frogmore tonight and poke around."

She gives me an uncertain look, but I pretend not to notice. I extend my hand to the closer of the two women standing in the doorway.

"Hi, I'm Rosemary."

"I'm Kelly. It's so nice to meet you."

We walk through the door while Thyme and her facialist get acquainted. As Kelly leads me to the treatment room, my mind is racing, running through how the rest of the afternoon and evening will go. The facials are our final treatments of the day. We'll shower, meet the guys for dinner, and then Thyme and I will make up an excuse to ditch the others so we can get to the bottom of the alleged wedding curse.

Once we find evidence that Trina Lyman's the evil spirit messing up Sage's wedding plans, we'll confront her and tell her she either stops immediately or we'll tell Roman and Sage. With any luck, she'll agree, and Sage will never have to know.

CHAPTER 15

Thyme

$\mathcal{I}$ close my eyes while Moriah applies a thick layer of green goop to my face. The seaweed and kelp mask sounded so refreshing when I chose it, but now I worry I'm going to smell like sushi when this is over.

Yum, sushi.

My stomach growls enthusiastically. The spa's restaurant is lovely and the salads were nourishing, fresh, and delicious. But the portions have to be a joke. You know those videos online where people make tiny food and serve it on dollhouse dishes? It was about a half a step away from that.

I distract myself from my gnawing hunger by thinking about Rosemary's wild accusation. I want to dismiss it as impossible, but I have to admit Sage's future mother-in-law doesn't seem overly excited about the impending nuptials. In contrast, Muffy's over the moon about it. Heck, even that Hunter lady seems more supportive than Trina.

I frown.

Moriah gives my arm a light slap. "No frowning. You'll end up with sad lines. If you have to have lines, smile lines are better."

I relax my mouth and smooth my expression.

"That's better." She finishes plastering the green stuff over my face and covers it with a warm, damp towel. "We'll leave this on for fifteen minutes then rinse and moisturize."

I return to my musing. Rosemary's theory is still pretty out there. But she actually said something important. Assuming there's not a cranky haint terrorizing Sage and Roman and there really is a person behind their string of bad luck, whoever took the rings had access to Roman's car keys. I'm not so sure we should go skulking around Frogmore tonight like Scooby-Doo and the gang. But asking Roman for a list of people who have access to his keys seems like a reasonable, and reasonably adult, next step.

My gurgling stomach protests.

Correction: driving through a fried chicken joint on the way home seems like a more pressing next step. But, after that, we talk to Roman about the keys. I hope against hope that he tells us his mom *doesn't* have keys to his car. I know Rosemary's firmly in the 'it's always better to know' camp. But, frankly, I see great psychological protective value in *not* knowing your future mother-in-law is so opposed to your union that she faked an evil spell.

Trapped in the salon chair, with my face covered, I have nothing better to do than ruminate. My mind inevitably follows the subject of weddings and mothers-in-law to a topic I try hard not to think about.

Everyone's waiting for Victor to pop the question. Everyone except for me, that is. Don't get me wrong. I love the guy. Can't imagine my life without him. Truly. And I'm sure we'll probably make it official ... someday. I just don't see any urgency.

For one thing, aside from his sister Helena, who lives in New York, I don't really know his family. We traveled to Brazil last summer and I met them, but it was a short visit. They were kind and welcoming, but they're basically strangers. I mean, for all I know, they have a whole slew of evil curses, hexes, and jinxes following them around. Unlikely, sure. But it just goes to show, I don't know what I don't know.

As I always do when the subject of marrying Victor bubbles to the surface, I reassure myself that this isn't something to worry about now. He hasn't asked me. But every once in a while he says something that makes it clear he thinks about it. And with the comments my mom and sisters have been making, there's no chance the topic won't come up at Sage's wedding. I envision my mother informing Victor about my aging eggs and groan.

Moriah materializes at my shoulder, lifts a corner of the towel, and peers down at me worriedly. "Is something wrong? Does it burn? Tingle?"

"Oh, no. Sorry. I was just thinking about … something."

"Well, it's time to take it off anyway. I'm glad you're not having an allergic reaction, though. Those can be brutal."

She wipes my face clean with fast, practiced motions. Then she applies an avocado oil-based moisturizer, explaining the importance of moisturizing by using gentle, upward strokes to avoid those sad frown lines.

Happily, the scent of the moisturizer makes me forget all about my disintegrating eggs. Unfortunately, my musings about my love life are replaced by a powerful craving for guacamole. I scrap my fried chicken plan and hope there's a good Mexican restaurant near Sage's house.

CHAPTER 16

Sage

*S*prawled out in the back seat of the rental car, I can see Rosemary's eyes drift up to the rearview mirror again. I hurriedly look away so we don't make eye contact. I really don't feel like talking.

From the passenger seat, Thyme clears her throat delicately. Then she twists around to look at me. "It's really not that bad. Honestly, it's hardly noticeable. Right, Rosemary?"

"Yeah, absolutely," Rosemary lies in a voice that's about two octaves higher than normal.

I don't bother to respond. Every inch of my face and neck, including my eyelids, is covered with red, raised welts and hives and my lips are ballooned and swollen like I received a collagen injection from a mad scientist. Who knew a person could develop a contact allergy to honey in her mid-twenties? Not me, that's for sure.

Once it becomes clear I'm not going to answer, Thyme tries again.

"They were really nice about it at the spa. I mean, they called and arranged for us to pick up your antihistamine at that drive-through pharmacy, and they let us leave through the employee entrance."

"I'm not exactly good advertising for Saltwater & Serenity's service, Thyme. They don't want anyone to see me as a matter of self-preservation." I finally break my vow of silence.

"Okay, that's a fair point," Thyme concedes.

"But, hey, they didn't charge us for your facial," Rosemary interjects. "That's something!"

For some reason, her excitement about this dubious silver lining makes me laugh. And laugh, and laugh some more.

"Um, Sage? You okay?"

"Yeah." I catch Rosemary's eye in the mirror and smile. "I am. It's not even that itchy anymore. I'm just really tired of bad things happening to me."

"I know, honey."

"Don't call me *honey* ever again."

"Stupid bee poop," Thyme deadpans.

This sets me off on another bout of uncontrollable laughter. From the front seat, I hear first Thyme and then Rosemary start to giggle, too.

When I can breathe again, I wipe the tears from my puffy red eyes. "I had a great time with you."

"Yeah, right." Rosemary shoots me a skeptical look.

"I did. The spa was amazing. Right up until my face exploded." I half-laugh, half-snort. I wonder if I'm teetering on the edge of hysteria. Because none of this is *that* funny.

Thyme must be thinking the same thing because she turns and searches my face before asking, in her best psychologist voice, "You know it's okay to not be okay, right?"

I nod, not trusting myself to speak. She reaches back and gives my arm a squeeze.

After a moment, Rosemary asks, "What do you want to do for

dinner? I'm assuming eating out isn't an option, but we can pick something up. Or I'd love to cook for everyone."

I exhale. "It would be fabulous if you'd make dinner for the six of us. Tomorrow."

Her smile falters and she keeps her eyes on the road. "Sure. So, takeout tonight?"

"I'm really not up for company. I just want to make myself a bowl of oatmeal then climb into bed."

Thyme opens her mouth to protest but I talk over her. "You guys should go out, though. And do me a favor and take Roman along. I just want to mope. By myself. For one night." It's the truest summation of how I feel that I can think of.

Thyme considers this request. Then she nods. "One night. Mope at will. But, tomorrow, you turn that frown upside down."

The hokey saying makes me smile a little, even now. "Thanks for understanding, you guys. I have the best sisters."

"Wrong. I do. Spend some of your moping time deciding what you'll have for dinner tomorrow, okay? I've seen the sad state of your pantry. I'm going to need to hit a market."

"I will," I promise.

"In the meantime," Thyme says, "is there a decent Mexican joint around here?"

CHAPTER 17

Rosemary

*W*e drop Sage off and hustle Dave and Victor out of her place in a hurry so she and Roman can have a few minutes of privacy before she boots him out to begin her night of solitude.

"Was she stung by bees or what?" Dave asks.

I cock my head at my detective husband. "What exactly do you think happens at a spa? She was getting a facial, not playing amateur beekeeper."

"She looks like she's been stung. And you said something about honey."

"She had an allergic reaction. You know all about those, right?" After all, we met when my boss died from anaphylactic shock after an allergic reaction.

"Why was she eating honey at a spa?" Victor wants to know.

"She wasn't eating it. It was on her face."

"Oh, but we're the ridiculous ones," Dave shoots back. "What did you put on your face, Thyme?"

"Seaweed. And avocado oil," she mumbles.

Victor guffaws.

"And you?" Dave turns to me.

I give him a cool look. "A coffee bean and brown sugar scrub."

I wait for the crack, but he manages to resist temptation. I can see his restraint comes at a cost. He's literally biting his fist to keep from blurting out whatever smart remark he's dying to say.

Thyme shakes her head at him and Victor. Then she points at Denise's ceramic casserole pan, which is tucked under my arm. "Why did you take that from Sage's place, anyway?"

"Returning it gives us an excuse to go to St. Helena Island," I answer out of the side of my mouth.

Victor shifts his weight. Dave checks his watch. Thyme's stomach growls.

"Jeez, you guys are impatient," I observe, feeling positively saintly.

Thyme glowers at me. Oh, she's *hangry,* all right. But before she can snap at me, Roman comes bounding down the stairs two at a time.

Sage, with her red, splotchy face partially hidden behind the door, waves goodbye to us.

"Thanks for letting me tag along," Roman says.

Victor punches him in the shoulder. "Are you kidding? We're stoked to have you join us."

Roman grins. He has a nice smile. "Okay. Sage said you're in the mood for Mexican. We should drive over to Luis's Table. It's not far, and he has the best carnitas in town."

Thyme, Victor, and Roman pile into his little VW bug. I slide the casserole dish onto the back seat of the rental car, and Dave and I pull out behind Roman.

"How was golf?"

"Better than the spa. I hit the ball pretty straight. We avoided the water and the sand for the most part. Chip gave us some really great pointers. And, best of all, nobody in our foursome was attacked by bees."

Again with the bees?

I twist my head to stare at him to see if he's serious. He's very much not serious. He's grinning broadly, brimming with unjustified pride in his weak joke. I just shake my head.

"I'll take you to a spa someday. You'll see what it's all about."

He slides a hand onto my thigh. "Maybe we should practice at home first. Massages, I think."

I try to focus on the road with limited success. His fingers trace light circles on my leg through the thin fabric of my skirt. I stare harder at the road and squeak, "That sounds like fun. But … um … getting pulled over for erratic driving doesn't. So maybe we save the couples massage for later tonight?"

He gives me an amused look but stills his hand. "Yes, ma'am. Although I'm not sure traffic enforcement is high on the local PD's priority list. On the way back from Chip's country club, right there on the main road through town, we passed a man driving a golf cart while setting off fireworks with one hand and shotgunning a beer with the other."

"Oh, you did not. You're making that up. He had to have been steering with at least one hand," I point out.

"Well done, my adorable amateur detective. You cracked the case. I may have exaggerated just a bit."

"Speaking of cases, did you happen to find the wedding rings somewhere on the golf course? I mean, not to second guess your investigative techniques, but I highly doubt you stumbled over them lying on a green."

He shakes his head. "You have a lot to learn about legwork. The best way to do it is to not do it."

I wait for clarification. It's not forthcoming. Instead, he examines his fingernails while he whistles through his teeth.

"Fine, I'll bite. Do want to share the meaning of that little Zen koan?"

"Oh, sure, since you asked so nicely. We played nine. Then we stopped at the turn for lunch."

"Okay."

"While we were sitting in the bar waiting for our burgers, several members came over to shoot the breeze with Chip."

I wish he'd get wherever he's going a little faster. "Okay. *And?*"

"And, my love, Chip introduced us, making sure to emphasize that I'm a detective and that Victor's a journalist. He didn't *say* we were investigating a rash of car break-ins at the club. But he also didn't say that we *weren't.*"

I flick my eyes away from the road. "I don't think one break-in constitutes a rash."

"Would this be a bad time to make a joke about Sage's face?"

"Yes."

"Thought so." He coughs. "Moving on. Eager to avoid another scandal so close on the heels of the whole blackmail/murder/cheating fiasco that roiled the club a few years back, the Vice President offered up the tapes from the security cameras."

"Wait. Chip's country club has surveillance cameras?"

"Installed after Fred Spears met his demise. Apparently their insurer demanded it. I guess one murdered member in the locker room is all it takes to get an establishment labeled as high risk."

"Go figure. So, did you see anything?"

"Nothing conclusive. Roman's car was parked toward the edge of the lot, near the driving range. The camera did pick up a person unlocking Roman's passenger car door about twenty minutes after he parked. The suspect leaned in, opened the glove compartment and removed a box, then locked up and walked away. The entire process took less than a minute, and the culprit never turned to face the camera."

"Like he knew it was there?"

"Possibly. But, again, given where the car was parked it might have been coincidence."

In front of me, Roman signaled that he was about to turn left into a parking lot crowded with cars. Still thinking about this new information, I followed suit.

"Oh, and one more thing," Dave added as I pulled into a parking space. "Your evil spirit's not a he. It's a she. We couldn't make out much. But we could tell that the person was an African-American woman."

CHAPTER 18

Thyme

The restaurant's fairly busy, but the hostess recognizes Roman as Chip's caddy and finds us a booth toward the back of the noisy bar area. Once we're all seated, a bowl of hot, greasy tortilla chips and an assortment of salsas and dips arrive with a round of waters and beers.

We dig into the chips. I'm munching away happily, impressed by the fresh guacamole, when someone steps on my foot under the table. I try to pull my foot back, but the stomper increases the pressure, which means it's Rosemary, and it's not an accident.

I shoot her a look that says *Can't a girl enjoy an appetizer and a cold one?*

She shoots me back one that says *No.*

I sigh and place my napkin on the table. Then I turn to Victor. "Can I squeeze by you? I need to visit the ladies' room."

"I'll come with you," Rosemary says. She leaps to her feet.

Her husband gives her a lazy smile. "You don't have to have a little secret chat, you know. Victor and Roman were there. They saw the footage."

Rosemary smiles tightly. "Sure." She sits back down.

I look around the table. "Since I'm apparently the only one who doesn't know what's going on here, does someone want to fill me in?"

Victor nods. "We spoke to some people at the country club. There's surveillance camera footage of an African-American woman breaking into Roman's car."

I can feel my eyes go wide. "That's great ... isn't it?" I tack on the question when I notice nobody seems to share my excitement.

"It's a lead. But not a particularly useful one. There are a lot of African-American women in South Carolina. And the video is grainy, blurry, and taken from a distance. Even if it could be enhanced, the woman, whoever she is, kept her back to the camera the whole time."

Victor's explanation is like a pin to the balloon of my enthusiasm.

"Oh." I deflate.

Rosemary glances at Roman, who's sitting in the middle of the U-shaped bench flanked by me and Victor on his left and her and Dave on his right. Then she arches an eyebrow at Dave and clears her throat. I recognize her expression and have a feeling that, in a minute, Dave's going to wish he'd kept his mouth shut and let her talk to me in private. I drop my eyes and stare at the salsa verde like it's the most fascinating thing I've ever seen.

"I don't know, Victor. I'd say it's a pretty good lead all the same."

Roman tilts his head. "How do you figure?"

"Well, for one thing, this mystery woman is someone who has access to your car keys. And she might have known where the security cameras are located. That should narrow it down a lot, right?"

"Yeah, I guess you're right."

She waits a beat. "Does anybody have an extra key—your mom, maybe?"

Smooth, Rosemary. Real smooth.

He blinks at her. "My mom?"

"I mean, if I lived in the same town as my mother, I'd probably give her my spare key."

She keeps her voice casual. Meanwhile, there's zero chance Rosemary would let our mother come within a hundred feet of her car. Mom's not known for her attention span, and her driving record is littered with tickets for blowing through red lights, parking in no parking zones, and more than her fair share of minor fender benders. But I say nothing. I'm more interested in what Roman's going to say next.

He shakes his head. "I don't think she does."

"What about your Aunt Denise?"

"No."

"Your grandmother?"

Rosemary at least has the decency to sound embarrassed about accusing his eighty-four-year-old grandmother of breaking into his car.

"Uh, no. The only other person who has a key to my car is your sister." He pushes his beer away, frowning.

"That's no help," Rosemary muses, apparently oblivious to the fact that she's upsetting Sage's fiancé.

Dave tries to unruffle Roman's feathers. "That's useful information. I'm *sure* Rosemary doesn't think any of your relatives took the rings. Right, Rosie?"

He turns his head and locks eyes with Rosemary until she chirps, "Right."

"But," he continues, "this woman on the tape got the key from somewhere. Since you still have your key, she must have lifted Sage's."

The muscles in Roman's jaw relax visibly and he nods. "I'll ask her."

He pulls out his phone to text Sage, and I take advantage of the moment to shake my head at Rosemary, who responds with a little shrug.

Roman glances up from the phone. "She's checking in her handbag now."

I settle in for a wait. Sage's purse is a wasteland of receipts, discarded lipsticks, and random bits and bobs that Skylar and Dylan give her. She's been known to pull a pinecone, a seashell, and a handful of sticks out of that thing to get to her wallet.

Victor drapes his arm around my shoulder and I snuggle into his chest.

"It's gone. Sage said her key is missing."

Against my cheek I can feel Victor's heart rate quicken. My reporter's caught the scent of a story.

"Ask her when was the last time she used it or remembers seeing it," he suggests.

Roman thumbs out the question on his phone.

"She knows she had my spare set of keys on Monday because she met me at my apartment after work and beat me there. She let herself in to wait for me."

"What did you two do that night?" Dave asks.

"We made a quick dinner, cleaned up the kitchen, and headed back to Hilton Head for ... a class."

"What kind of class?"

"Uh, ballroom dancing." A faint pink stain peeks out from under his dark skin.

"Sure, for the wedding," I say encouragingly. "That's nothing to be embarrassed about."

"It kind of is. We're not very good. No, actually, we suck. So, we take the regular class on Mondays, and on Wednesdays we have our own private, remedial lesson. Madame Lucille says we're bad advertising for her services, so she threw in the private lessons for free so we don't humiliate ourselves and her during our first dance."

Victor swallows a laugh and I dig an elbow into his side.

"Sorry, man," he mumbles.

"It's okay. We're getting better."

"So, Monday was the group class?" Rosemary brings us back to the topic at hand.

"Right."

"How many couples are in your class?"

He blinks at the ceiling for a moment, clearly counting in his head. "Seven other couples."

"Are any of the other brides-to-be African-American?"

He shakes his head. "Actually, no." He waits a beat. "Madame Lucille is, but she would never—"

"Never say never," Dave intones.

Roman frowns. "Madame Lucille's the most proper, dignified woman you can imagine. There's no way she took Sage's keys. Besides, there's a row of hooks and cubbies in the hallway outside the studio. Everyone leaves their bags and shoes and stuff out there during class, and Madame Lucille never leaves the classroom during the lesson. She didn't have access or opportunity or whatever."

"But anybody could have walked in from the street and grabbed them?" I ask.

"I guess. But, they'd have to know we were there, know Sage has a set of my keys, know that I would be picking up the rings on Wednesday, *and* know that I'd be at the club that afternoon. On Monday, *I* didn't even know the rings would be ready on Wednesday. No, it had to have happened later. Or whoever took them is following me everywhere I go."

Dave agrees. "This wasn't some random purse snatcher. And there's nothing else missing from Sage's bag, is there?"

"She said no."

"There's probably not a big demand for seashells and stones on the black market," Rosemary says in a dry tone.

I cough to cover my giggle.

"Roman has a good point," Victor says. "If someone took the keys during dance class, she—or he—must be watching him and Sage."

A chill runs down my spine and goosebumps rise on my arms. Victor's sister had a stalker a few years ago, and the entire episode was terrifying. The creepy image of someone following Sage around the island, dogging her footsteps and spying on her, takes hold in my brain. My mouth goes dry.

Beside me, Victor laces his fingers through mine and squeezes my hand as if he knows what's running through my mind.

"None of the other students stepped out of the room during the class? Maybe to use the bathroom or take a phone call?" Dave asks in an even voice.

Roman scrunches up his face. "Not that I can remember."

I free my hand from Victor's and stand up. "We have to get the check and go. Now." My voice shakes.

Rosemary tilts her head and gives me a quizzical look. But Dave nods. "Right. Roman, will you call Chip and ask him to go over to Sage's until we get there?"

Understanding dawns in Rosemary's eyes and her face goes white. "Whoever took Roman's keys had access to Sage's, too."

Roman scrambles to his feet. Victor leans across me and places his hand on Roman's arm. "Remember, though, she has her keys and she said nothing else is missing. Don't panic."

He's right. But at the same time whoever took those keys could have taken Sage's, made a copy, and returned them to her purse. Unlikely? Sure. But not impossible.

"He's right. There's no reason to run off half-cocked. But I don't think Sage should spend the night at her place. Certainly not alone." Dave uses an authoritative, law enforcement tone.

It has the immediate effect of calming me down. Judging by the tightness around Roman's eyes, it's not a universal panacea, but he nods, swallows hard, and lifts the phone to his ear to talk to Chip.

I realize we haven't eaten dinner, just a bunch of chips and salsa. But it doesn't matter now. My appetite's vanished, replaced by a lump of fear and dread that settles in my stomach like a too-heavy meal.

CHAPTER 19

Sage

$\mathcal{I}$ crack the door open wide enough to peer out at Chip.

"I don't need a bodyguard," I assure him. I leave unsaid the fact that if I *did* need one, Chip Moore wouldn't be on my short list. He's a nice guy and all, but he's not exactly menacing.

"Just until your sisters get back."

"I appreciate your coming over here. I really do. But I'm not in any danger. Besides, if anyone comes to the cottage, they'll have to drive right past the main house to get here. You'll see them."

Unless they approach the property from the beach path behind the guest cottage.

I ignore the ominous voice in my head and smile at Chip. He doesn't smile back.

"Not if they come up from the beach path," he says.

Okay, that's creepy, I'm forced to admit to myself.

I sigh and pull the door wide open. "Come on in."

Before he can step inside, I see Muffy running through her

garden, cutting across the lawn to reach my cottage faster. Chip turns.

"What's the matter?" he asks as she hurries up the stairs. "Is it one of the kids?"

"The kids are fine. They're watching 'Mary Poppins' in the family room and spilling popcorn all over the carpet, no doubt. I overheard your call with Roman. You go on back to the house. I'll stay with Sage until he gets here."

Chip opens his mouth to protest but Muffy steamrolls over him. "Look at her, Chip. She's tired, she's injured, and she has an unpleasant rash. She doesn't want to sit around and make awkward small talk with her future father-in-law in her condition. She'd probably almost rather risk an attack."

It's not like she's *wrong*.

She smiles winningly up at her husband. "We'll have a cup of tea and some girl talk until Roman and her sisters get back. You can play sentry from the house."

"Well ..." he looks around like the answer might be written somewhere handy.

He hesitates, but all three of us know that what Muffy wants, Muffy gets.

"We'll be fine," I chime in. "Muffy's more of a badass than you realize."

She grins. "It's true."

"It probably is." He bends and brushes her lips with a soft kiss. When he straightens up, he searches out my eyes. "I'm going to sit out on the veranda and have a nightcap. I'll be able to see the street and if someone comes around from the back on foot."

I nod.

Muffy slips under his arm and into the cottage apartment. Then she pushes her arms against his chest and he takes a step back.

"See you in a bit," she trills before closing the door on him.

"Now, how about that tea? You get comfy on the couch and I'll bring it in."

She bustles over to the kitchen and starts filling the kettle before I can even respond, so I do as she says and get myself situated with a stack of pillows under my left leg.

When the water's ready she tosses some teabags into a couple of mugs and carries them over to the couch.

"I took the liberty of making yours chamomile. You need to get some decent sleep," she says as I take the mug in both hands.

"Thanks, Muffy."

She smiles. "My pleasure. Now, I'm gonna use some of your honey in my tea. I assume you don't want any."

"No, no more honey for me. Ever. In fact, take that jar home with you if you want it."

She settles herself in my armchair with a thoughtful expression on her face. "It's so odd that you developed a contact allergy to honey all of a sudden. But, you know, the hives are going down. Your face is looking better already."

I sip my tea. I open my mouth, think better of what I'm about to say, and close it.

"What is it, Sage? Are you worried about this stalker person?"

"Do you believe in curses?" I blurt.

"Curses?"

"Hexes, spells, jinxes, bad juju. Whatever you want to call it."

She considers the question for a long moment. "I can't say I do. Why, do you?"

I lift one shoulder. "Maybe."

"Contact dermatitis after a pricy facial stinks, but I don't think it's evidence you've been hexed."

"It's not the rash. Or at least, not *just* the rash."

"Talk to me, Sage. We're friends."

We are friends. But she's also my boss. And my future step-mother-in-law. On the one hand, there's no need for her to think I'm bananas. On the other hand, she's one of the smartest, savviest women I've ever met. And she's lived here a long time. She understands the local customs and cultures.

I take a deep breath and plunge into my story. "Roman's family has a long-running feud with another Frogmore family—The Davises."

She shakes her head. She's never heard of them.

"The short version of the story is that generations ago a Lyman daughter and a Davis son were betrothed. He got another woman pregnant, and they married. His family shunned his new bride because they wanted him to marry Betsy Lyman. His wife, in turn, blamed the Lymans for her troubles and raised her children to hate them. Also, she taught them to spellcast or whatever the Gullah/Geechee equivalent is."

"Probably, she raised them to be root doctors. Root women still help out as midwives and doulas at births in the Lowcountry. And Root men function as herbalists, more or less."

I think of the binding love spell Denise gave me. "So, if I wanted a mix of herbs, is there a store I could go to on St. Helena?"

"Oh, I don't know about a storefront. My guess would be you'd ask someone who knows someone who knows someone."

"Hmm."

"There, I mean. On St. Helena. But here, you just need to keep your eyes open. Pretty much any natural foods store or yoga studio that sells aromatherapy candles probably also has some traditional poultices and root cures premade on the shelves. They'd just be packaged and marketed to a different crowd. But what's this have to do with you being cursed?"

"Roman's grandmother thinks a Davis descendant cursed our wedding. Or maybe she thinks the original curse all those years ago carried forward. I'm not sure. But, you have to admit, there's a cloud over the wedding."

"You mean because your dress shop went out of business and the rings were stolen?"

"Among other things. It makes me wonder about evil spirits."

Muffy frowns. "But the security footage from the club shows a woman breaking into Roman's car. Someone with a key. I'm no authority on spirits and ghosts, but I'm pretty sure they don't need keys."

"That's fair." I concede the point.

"It's clear someone wants to throw a wrench into your wedding plans. But I'd start with living, breathing people. Women. Does Roman have an old girlfriend who might still be carrying a torch?"

"Not that I know of."

Muffy bites her lower lip, as if she's trying to decide whether to say something.

"What is it?"

"I'm just wondering why you're so reluctant to take Hunter up on her offer? It would solve a lot of problems. And Chip and I have told Roman multiple times that we can help financially."

I'm really not up for a heart-to-heart about Roman's extended family and Muffy's place in it. Or about the cultural and socioeconomic differences between St. Helena and Hilton Head. But this conversation has to happen sometime.

"It's complicated. I don't want Roman's family to think he's turning his back on his heritage by marrying me."

"Why on earth would they?"

"You've been to St. Helena, right?"

She bristles. "Of course I have. The Junior League has a partnership with the ladies' auxiliary at Second Baptist. That's how I met Denise. That's how Roman came to work for Chip."

"Okay. So, you can see how a wedding ceremony at Second Baptist with an outdoor reception after would have a different atmosphere than one that takes place at your country club. I mean, you do, right?"

Understanding blooms on her face. "But that's why Hunter's

the perfect person to help you! She's a bridge between the two cultures."

"Hunter Redforth?" Surely Muffy's not suggesting that simply because Hunter's African-American, she understands Frogmore. Oprah Winfrey's also a Black woman. But that doesn't mean she fathoms St. Helena Island's culture. Well, *she* might. I mean, it's Oprah.

"Yes, Hunter."

I'm almost afraid to ask. "Why?"

I brace myself for her to say something so shockingly ignorant that it shatters my image of her forever. What she says shatters one image, but it's not hers.

"She grew up on St. Helena Island."

I realize my mouth's hanging open. I clamp my jaw shut. "Really? I just assumed ..."

"You assumed she came from a wealthy, connected family."

"Well, yeah." My cheeks blaze. I, of all people, ought to know better than to make assumptions about how anyone grew up. I shake my head, confused. "But she's about my age. I wonder why Roman doesn't know her, like from high school or something."

"She did mention once that her parents split up when she was in middle school, and she and her mom moved to Beaufort. While they were living there, her mother met and married Jerome Redforth, who was an up-and-coming banker. About a year later, the Redforths moved to Charlotte, North Carolina. Hunter's mom and stepfather still live there. But she moved back to the area after college."

"Hmm."

"Yeah."

We drink our tea in companionable silence for a few moments. I'm not at all sure what to make of Muffy's story about Hunter. But maybe she *is* the answer to my wedding troubles. Muffy's cell phone sounds a few bars of a song that I don't know but that I recognize as her special Chip ringtone.

"Yes … okay … I will … strawberry."

She ends the call and looks at me. "Roman just pulled into the driveway. Chip told him you two are welcome to spend the night in the guest room but he declined. If you change your minds, just come over. We'll have your locks changed in the morning."

"It's probably not necessary. I really doubt this mystery woman made a copy of my key. Honestly."

"Better safe than sorry." She stands, gives me a kiss on the cheek, and heads to the kitchen with the mugs.

"Thanks for the company," I say over my shoulder. "Enjoy your shake."

A mischievous grin spreads across her face. Skylar's developed an allergy of her own—to dairy—so as a show of solidarity the entire Moore family is ostensibly lactose-free. But on Friday nights, after the kids are asleep, Chip runs down to the Island Diner and orders two of their famous milkshakes for takeout, and he and Muffy indulge in their thick, creamy, dairy vice.

She waves goodbye as Roman's car comes to a stop outside and the sound of the engine dies. I hear them greeting each other on the stairs outside the apartment.

The weight of the day's drama hits me full-on, and I'm asleep before Roman even steps inside.

CHAPTER 20

Rosemary

The bombshell about the key plays right into my plans. Roman's in a hurry to get back to Sage, so he eagerly takes me up on my offer for the four us to swing by his apartment and get him a change of clothes—you know, since we're headed to St. Helena anyway, to return his Aunt Denise's casserole dish. He hands his house key over and speeds off for the cottage.

Victor volunteers to drive the rental car out to Frogmore, which suits me fine. I settle against the back seat and twist my back from side to side to loosen my spine. Dave leans over and pokes me in the side while I'm mid-stretch.

"Ow! What was that for?"

"I want to know what you're up to."

"Just trying to loosen up. My back's tight."

"No, Rosemary, not the car calisthenics, why are—?"

"Actually, calisthenics exercises are things like pushups, pull ups, squats. The sort of stretch she's doing … sorry." Thyme trails off when she realizes nobody else cares about her personal trainer pedantry.

Dave tries again. "Why is it some sort of urgent emergency to return a casserole dish?"

"It's a chef thing. You wouldn't understand."

Thyme snorts and twists around to talk to Dave. "It's an excuse to go to Frogmore to spy on Roman's family."

I shoot her my best death glare. She's the worst partner for a secret mission, what with the meaning of the word *secret* apparently eluding her. Beside me, my husband shakes his head as if he's disappointed, but not surprised. I spare a death glare for him, too.

"And we're spying on the Lymans why?" Victor asks.

"Look, I don't *want* Roman's mom to be the person trying to sabotage the wedding. But everyone except Sage agrees there's no curse, right?"

"Actually, there *is* a curse. That's beyond dispute," Victor insists.

"What?"

"Sure. At some point, one of the Davises did curse the Lyman family. Whether that curse has ever had any effect … well that's a different issue."

I think on this for a few seconds and decide it's a distinction without a difference. But there's no point in arguing the issue with Victor. So I choose my next words with care and move on.

"Okay. Can we all agree there's a living person messing up the plans? Sure, maybe she's acting at the behest of a hundred-some-year-old spell, but she's *real.* Right?"

"Sure." Victor shrugs.

"And I think we start with the women in Roman's family."

"What kind of relatives do you think he has?" Dave wonders.

"The same kind as the rest of us—the flawed, imperfect kind. People do strange things. Does anyone in this car *really* want to argue differently?"

A silence falls as we all consider the murderers, abusers, blackmailers, and sociopathic criminals who've crossed our paths.

"Didn't think so. So here's the plan. Drop me and Thyme off at Denise's and go get Roman's stuff from his place. We'll ask Denise to give us a lift into town. Sage said Denise has some committee meeting at the cultural center at eight o'clock, so she can drop us off on her way. There's a bookstore with a café that's open late. We'll meet you there."

"Works for me. But don't you want to talk to Roman's mom?" Dave wants to know.

"She's still at work," I explain.

Victor asks Thyme to pull up the directions to Denise's house. I settle back in my seat and smile to myself. Trina Lyman *is* working late. But the department store where she works is right across the street from the bookstore. Thyme and I can pop in for a surprise visit after we talk to Denise.

Do I feel guilty omitting this small detail from my conversation with Dave and Victor? Nope. Not even a tiny bit. They may be a homicide detective and an investigative journalist, but here's a little secret about men: they can't look at a mother, anybody's mother, with clear eyes. My scientific hypothesis is that it's hardwired into their DNA. Mom is right up there with apple pie and the world's most boring pastime—seriously, seven innings would be plenty!

Luckily, I harbor no such illusions about the infallibility of maternal types.

DENISE IS surprised to see us, and maybe not entirely pleased. But she covers it well and ushers us into her cozy home and straight back to the kitchen.

"Do you girls drink coffee? tea? lemonade? Something stronger?"

"A glass of water would be great," Thyme says.

Denise purses her mouth disapprovingly at this breach of the unspoken code of Southern hospitality but fills a glass from the water dispenser built into her refrigerator and hands it to Thyme.

"Thank you."

"What about you, Rosemary?"

I give her the casserole dish and my biggest smile. "Lemonade sounds perfect."

She nods as she takes the dish. "Thanks for returning this, but really there was no need to make a special trip."

I wait until she's poured two glasses of lemonade from a pitcher in the fridge and we've all settled into chairs around the kitchen table to say, "Actually, we didn't make a special trip."

"Oh?"

I take a sip and watch her face. "No, Dave and Victor dropped us off on their way to Roman's apartment."

"Guys' night?"

"Nothing quite so pleasant, I'm afraid. It looks like that old Davis curse reared its head again."

Thyme's eyes go wide but she just sips her water.

Denise jerks her head back. "Is Sage still going on about that curse?"

"She had an allergic reaction to her facial today," Thyme volunteers.

"Oh my."

"Yeah. She really doesn't want Roman to see her looking all blotchy and red—"

"Shoot, now, he knows he wants to be her husband. He knows marriage means seeing her at her best and at her worst."

She's got a point.

"True enough."

"Would a conjurer be able to cause a rash like Sage's? Hives, welts, that sort of thing."

She cocks her head. "Are you asking me if *I* think a conjurer hexed your sister? If so, I'll tell you girls what I told her. I don't believe in folk magic. But I don't rule out the possibility that *someone's* cursed the kids, if you catch my drift."

"So you're agnostic on the subject?" Thyme clarifies.

Roman's aunt presses her lips together in a thin line. A small vee creases her forehead. "I wouldn't put it that way. To my way of thinking, agnostic's another way of saying too cowardly to commit. No, I'm saying someone who does believe in spells and charms might have it out for the Lymans—or Roman and Sage, specifically." She sips her lemonade.

She's basically taking the same position as Victor: a curse may not be causing any of Sage's current problems, but someone may have taken the trouble to aim one at her.

"But, if that's how you feel … why did you give Sage that spirit tree?" Thyme wants to know.

"That's a fair a question. Look, *I* don't believe. But I think your sister might. I didn't see any harm in giving her the tree. I figured it might ease her mind, and it would let the person who's cursed her know she's protected. That's why I have a bottle tree in my own yard."

She's lost me. "Sorry?"

"You know how white folks sometimes put up a sign on their door that says their home's monitored by an alarm company or a Beware of Dog sign even if they don't have a home security system or a vicious dog?"

I'm not so sure this ploy is limited to white people, but I know what she's talking about. "Yeah?"

Thyme's nodding her understanding. "Right. Or the way single women in New York might use a male name on their apartment buzzer label."

"Sure," Denise agrees. "It doesn't require much of you, but

maybe it encourages the bad actor —or the bad spirit, as the case may be—to move on to somebody else's house." She shrugs. "So that's why I gave your sister the bottle tree."

"Do you know who would have it out for Roman and Sage?"

"You're asking about members of the Davis family? I can't say I do. Your generation is pretty far-flung, not too many young people decide to stay in the Lowcountry when they're ready to start jobs and families. And the folks my age and older ... those Davises aren't really committed to the feud anymore." She shakes her head sadly, as if she's bemoaning the loss of a good, old-fashioned feud.

The clock hanging over the kitchen sink chimes the hour. She eyes it, drains her glass of lemonade, and gives us an apologetic smile. "I don't like to be a bad hostess, but I've got a meeting in town to get to. It's an important one—we're finalizing the details for tomorrow's citizens' archeological dig at the old ruins."

I'm only half-listening. This is our cue, but I still haven't pressed her about the keys. There's something imposing about Roman's petite Aunt Denise.

Thyme carries her glass over to the sink. "Thanks for the water. Can we hitch a ride into town with you?"

"Of course. Oh, and you can do me a favor, too. I have something else for Sage. Just let me put my face on and we'll go." She bustles out of the room to get ready.

Thyme turns to me. "What happened to your bad cop routine?"

I don't answer. She flashes a knowing smile.

"Yeah, I'm kind of afraid of her, too."

I smother a giggle.

Denise sweeps back into the room with her makeup in place and a smart hat pinned to her hair. She's carrying a large white dress bag.

"It that ... Sage's wedding gown?" Thyme asks.

"It surely is."

"How did you—?"

"I stopped by Jessalyn's house on my way home. She's still out of town taking care of some family matters and I figured her husband Nate could use a home-cooked meal. We got to talking about Jessalyn's business troubles. He mentioned that all Jessalyn's inventory that was at the boutique was tied up in the financial mess, but I happen to know she has a habit of bringing her more complicated projects home where she can work on them without interruption. I figured a wedding dress might fit the bill, so I asked if I could peek in her sewing room while Nate ate his chicken and rice. Sure enough, Sage's gown was hanging on a dress form with the pins still in the hem."

"And you just *took* it?" I try to keep my voice neutral. I'm not sure I succeed.

"I tried to pay him for it, of course. But he got on the phone with Jessalyn and she forbade him to take my money. She said she didn't finish the job and that if the dress was there when she got home, she'd have to, in good conscience, turn it over to the bankruptcy court or some such. But if it was gone …" She raises both eyebrows.

"Sage is going to be so happy! Thank you," I enthuse.

"It's my absolute pleasure, dear. I'm heartsick about all the troubles the kids have been having. We all are."

"We?"

"Well my mama and Roman's mama are both tied in knots over this mess, too." She leans in conspiratorially and continues, "In fact, I've sicced Effie on Reverend Walker. How that man thinks he can just back out of officiating the wedding because he's got the chance to address the Hilton Head Interfaith Council … it's not right. My mother'll set him straight. You just wait and see."

If Granny Effie is anything like her daughter, I have no doubt she will.

"What about Trina?" I ask, faux casually.

"What about her?" Denise wrinkles her forehead at the question.

"Does she have any ideas about how we can get the wedding back on track?" Thyme interjects quickly, as if she's afraid of what I may say in response.

"Mmm. I can't say I've talked much to her lately. She's so busy with work."

This squares with what Sage told us. I keep my face blank. I don't want to pass judgment on a woman for being busy with work. But it seems like her son and future daughter-in-law could use a hand.

Denise has a faraway look in her eyes. Then she blinks like she's just remembered something. "Of course, she's got something up her sleeve. She told me she has a surprise for the kids."

"A surprise?"

"I don't know the details. The only reason I know she's planning something is she needed my help."

"What kind of help?" I ask.

Denise sucks air through her teeth, thinking. After a moment, she makes up her mind. "I suppose there's no harm in telling you. Especially since I don't actually know anything. She asked me to try to get Roman's car keys without him noticing."

My heart lodges itself in my throat, blocking me from speaking. I throw Thyme a desperate look.

"Did you succeed?" she asks.

"Heavens, no. How would I even manage that?"

My heart thuds back into my chest and a veil of disappointment falls over me like someone's lowered a curtain. Denise's next words lift the curtain and set my pulse hammering.

"I couldn't see a way to get his keys, so I did the next best thing. I knew Sage would have those kids of Chip's at the nature center on Tuesday morning. They love those programs. So I 'bumped' into them there and sneaked Sage's spare set out of her handbag. Which, let me tell you was no easy task. Who on earth carries seagull feathers and plastic baggies of *sand* in her purse?" She shakes her head in amazement.

Thyme and I manage a pair of weak laughs as we follow Denise out onto the porch. I hold the dress while she locks up her house. The whole time, Thyme and I are exchanging meaningful stares behind her back.

I cannot *wait* to hear what Trina Lyman has to say for herself.

CHAPTER 21

Sage

I dream that Roman and I are having milkshakes in big, old-fashioned drugstore glasses shaped like goblets. My glass is heavy in my hand, and I notice viscous amber liquid swirled into the vanilla base.

Butterscotch syrup, I think.

But then I taste the cloying sweetness and realize with horror that it's honey.

My throat constricts. Smaller, tighter. It's closing. I can't breathe.

I drop the shake to claw at my throat and the thick glass crashes to the tile floor. The deafening shatter echoes as milk, honey, and ice cream splatter everywhere. Cold flecks hit my face as I gulp, fish-like, desperate for air.

I start awake on the couch, gasping. My hair is plastered to my forehead with sweat. Heart still racing, I push the stray strands back from my face and struggle upright.

I inhale, long and slow, and assure myself I can breathe. *I am breathing.*

The clock over the stove glows in the dim room. The luminous red numbers read 7:52.

I remember dozing off as Muffy was leaving. But where's Roman? He wouldn't be in bed this early. It's not even eight o'clock.

I listen for a moment. Through the bathroom door at the end of the hall I hear the faint, muffled patter of my shower running. A rectangle of yellow light leaks out from under the door.

That mystery solved, I sit back, still catching my breath after the disturbing dream. That's when I hear it again—the tinkle of glass smashing against the ground.

It takes me several seconds to understand that the breaking glass isn't a dream sound. It's coming from outside, in the garden.

I half-roll, half-fall off the couch. In the process, I manage to bang my left shin hard against the coffee table. The tortured noise I make is somewhere between a yelp and a mewl.

I scramble to my feet, hoping like hell I haven't torn open my stitches thanks to my ungraceful dismount. From outside comes the noise of more broken glass raining down.

I limp-run to the balcony and squint out into the dark. From the direction of the sound, I think the glass is hitting against the stepping stones that wind a path from the garden bench to my front steps. I press my face against the sliding glass door.

A dark shape slips out from behind the crepe myrtle and hurls a handful of stones. The rocks hit the spirit tree and at least one more glass bottle explodes. I strain to make out details but the figure is just a shadow.

Hot anger spreads across my chest suffocating my initial icy fear. I don't think. I just race over to the front door, throw the lock open, and hurl myself down the stairs, shouting wordlessly at the punk in my garden.

I'm unsteady on my feet—a combination of stiffness from the wound site, residual pain from cracking my leg against the coffee table, and inborn clumsiness. I lose my footing on the third step from the bottom and land in a heap on the concrete patio at the base of the stairs.

My vandal whirls around and takes off running toward the beach path. The movement activates the motion-sensing light mounted on the far left corner of the guest cottage. I get one glimpse as the person passes under the light. I can't make out her features, but I can see that it's a woman. She has dark skin, and her hair's tucked up under a baseball cap.

"Hey, I want to talk to you!" I shout at her disappearing back as I pull myself to my feet and take off after her. She's not hobbled and bleeding and has a decent lead on me. She's gone before I reach the corner of the cottage.

I pull up short and turn back to the garden to assess the damage.

When Roman emerges from the shower, he sees the front door swinging open and panics. He rushes outside wearing nothing but a towel wrapped around his waist and finds me kneeling in a sea of jagged cobalt glass, scooping the broken pieces into a pile while tears run down my cheeks.

"Hey, hey, it's okay," he soothes as he gently guides me to standing. "Give me that." He takes the shards of glass from my hands, places them on the garden bench, and pulls me close.

I press my tear-stained face to his bare chest. His skin is hot and he smells like my lemongrass and litsea soap. I inhale shakily.

"Did you see the jerk who did this? Did you recognize him?"

"It was a woman. I didn't see her face," I mumble.

He tightens his arms around me. "You're not hurt are you?"

I take a quick inventory. My left leg is definitely bleeding, I can feel the wetness spreading across the gauze dressing—the stitches have probably pulled open. My hands are dirty from scrabbling around in the dirt. And my heart's still thumping like an overenthusiastic golden retriever's tail. But, I'm okay.

I'm madder than hell. But I'm okay.

I nod.

He lifts my chin with a finger and searches my eyes.

"You know this doesn't mean anything, right?"

I tilt my head, confused.

"What doesn't mean anything?"

"The broken bottles."

I shake my head from side to side, still not comprehending. "What would it mean?"

He huffs out a breath, pressing his lips together in an expression of self-disgust. "I shouldn't have said anything."

"Roman—"

"If a bottle breaks, the spirit trapped inside escapes. I mean, that's what people believe," he mumbles reluctantly.

I spend about ten seconds considering the horror scenario of a mass of evil spirits spinning around us like sandstorms, then I shake my head. "Yeah, I'm not really worried about evil spirits at this point. I'm more concerned with the corporeal being who's running around causing trouble."

Relief floods his face. "That's good news."

"You have a weird definition of good news."

He cracks a smile, but it fades quickly. "We need to get you inside and clean up your leg."

"What about this mess? We can't leave it like this. Skylar or Dylan might wander out here." I gesture uncertainly at the broken glass carpeting the ground.

"Aren't they in bed by now? We'll clean it up in the morning when it's light out." He drops his gaze to his towel. "And when I'm wearing clothes."

"That's fair," I concede.

"Good."

We walk up the stairs side by side, and he keeps an arm firmly circled around my back, as if I might topple over backward. Of course, having managed to injure myself three times in the past two days, I can't say I blame him.

Inside, I remove the blood-soaked dressing and clean my leg

while Roman calls Dave to get his thoughts as to whether we should report the vandalism to the police. I think so, but Roman's less sure. So we agree that Detective Dave should be the tiebreaker.

Roman ends the call and looks at me with a pained expression.

"Well? What'd he say?"

He doesn't answer me.

"Roman?"

"He said we can wait to call in the morning. They're unlikely to send someone out to take a statement tonight."

"Okay. Did he say anything else? You look like you're worried about something."

"He said your sisters are off playing amateur sleuth."

"What are they up to?"

"He didn't know exactly. He and Victor are supposed to meet them in about thirty minutes, and then they'll all come here."

"Meet them where? Where are they?"

He pulls a face. "Frogmore."

I swear under my breath. Rosemary and Thyme mean well—I know they do. But they don't know Frogmore or the people. I just know this little investigation of theirs will end in disaster.

Does it ever.

CHAPTER 22

Thyme

*D*enise drops us off at the bookstore café and heads to her committee meeting. We wave our goodbyes, and I follow Rosemary on autopilot into the shop.

"Do you want to get some tea or something?"

I nod. Sure. Maybe some caffeine will clear my head. Ever since Denise shared her bombshell about Roman's mom, I've felt like I'm in a trance. My brain is fuzzy. I can't seem to focus on anything other than the fact that Trina Lyman got her hands on Sage's keys and broke into her own son's car to steal the wedding rings.

Who *does* that?

A sharp poke in my ribs interrupts my musing.

"Ow!" I glare at Rosemary and rub my side.

"This gentleman's waiting for you to order," she says in an overly sweet and patient voice.

I give my head a little shake and blink a few times. "Sorry."

The African-American man behind the counter smiles, unbothered by my spaceyness. I glance around. The bookstore is nearly empty and there's no sign of other employees. He appears to be running both the café counter and the bookstore single-handedly.

"What'll it be for you, little lady?" His patois is thick and his rich voice rumbles like a bass guitar.

I scan the chalkboard hanging on the wall behind him. At this hour, I really should stick with herbal tea or chai latte. But my brain is still on the fritz from learning that Roman's mom is the wedding saboteur. I need something stronger.

"Espresso, please. A double."

His eyebrows creep up a notch but he nods. "You got it."

"You're going to be up all night," Rosemary warns.

"Don't remember asking for your opinion," I snap back at her.

My adrenaline is still spiked from the revelation about Trina, and it doesn't take much for that energy to morph into anger. I need to reset. I take a long slow breath in through my nose—*one, two, three, four*. Then I hold the breath for a seven-count before releasing it through my mouth for a long, *whooshing* eight-count.

Rosemary and the man behind the counter watch me.

"Feeling better?" she asks.

"Yes. Thanks." The breathing technique works like a charm to stave off anxiety and panic, if you repeat the cycle four times. I just need one breathing cycle to get a grip on my crankiness.

The man behind the counter eyes me closely. "Do you girls need anything else?"

"I think we're all set." I smile at him and turn to Rosemary. "My treat."

I pay for our drinks, and we carry them to a small table set up in the window that runs most of the length of the side wall of the building. We have a clear view of Dixon's Department Store, which sits just on the other side of a narrow alley. Presumably, we'll be able to see when Trina Lyman leaves work.

And then? I have no idea what Rosemary has planned. I catch her eye across the table.

"I guess you were right about Roman's mom."

"Maybe. We'll see what she has to say."

I nearly spew hot coffee on her. "Hang on a minute. Earlier, you were convinced she was pure evil, now you want to *wait and see*? Her own sister just said she asked her to get the keys."

"Right. Which makes me wonder."

"Wonder about what?"

"If you were planning to do something like that, would you ask me for help?"

I consider the question. "I might."

She gives a small nod then juts her chin out. "Yeah, I might, too. But you know what else I'd do? I'd make darn sure you know not to tell anybody."

Okay, she has a point. But maybe Trina lied to her sister. Or *maybe* Denise is in on it. I reject this idea as soon as it flits across my mind. She's clearly a huge fan of Sage's. She rescued her wedding gown, for crying out loud. My eyes drift toward the dress bag, draped carefully over the back of an empty chair. None of this makes any flipping sense.

"So, what are you saying?"

"I'm not sure. But there's no way Denise would've helped her steal the wedding rings. And, for sure, she wouldn't have given her the keys if she thought she was going to do something rotten. Denise said Trina's planning a surprise. So ..."

"So?"

"So, we're just going to ask her."

"What? Just say 'hey, why did you want the keys to Roman's car?'"

"Yep."

She falls silent and resumes her stakeout, watching the entrance to Dixon's through the window.

I sip my strong, bitter coffee. After a few minutes, I grow restless. Staring out a window isn't much fun when there are no people to watch. And the street appears to be nearly deserted. I get up and wander around the bookstore.

There's a small section of shelves devoted to gifts. Candles, journals, fancy pens. And on the bottom shelf, a neat row of small red flannel sacks. I crouch and read the shelf tag: *Root bags, assorted. Ask for pricing.*

Root bags. I pick one at random and balance it in the palm of my hand. It's heavier than it looks, about the weight of a medium apple. There's no writing on the bag to provide any hint of its contents. I sniff it. I get a whiff of something astringent, almost menthol.

"Do you have any questions?"

I jump and nearly go over backward on my butt. The man from the coffee counter smiles and offers me a hand, which I gratefully, if not gracefully, accept.

"Didn't mean to startle you," he says as he helps me to my feet.

"No, it's okay. I was daydreaming." I'm still clutching the root bag. "What is this stuff?"

"Well, let me see, now."

He extends his hand and I drop the bag into it. He peers through the bottom half of his glasses at the cloth, raises it to his nose, and inhales deeply.

"Ah, this here is sage. Good for reversing spells and warding off misfortune."

Sage? Out of all those bags, I picked sage?

"Just sage?"

A flash of irritation crosses his face. "We don't sell premade bags here. You'll have to look elsewhere if that's what you're after."

"Oh, no, no. I'm not looking for anything. I just … I don't know anything about hoodoo …" I trail off helplessly.

His face softens. "Well, these bags are for root workers who have some experience. But, if you're interested in the topic, we have a selection of titles that'll give you some good background information. Many of them were written by local authors. Here, I'll show you the local interest section."

He leads me to a display and points out a handful of books. I flip through a few and end up choosing *Lowcountry Root Work and Conjuring: A History with Recipes.* I follow him back to the front counter to pay for my new reading material. He's still holding the bag of sage.

"Could I get the sage, too?" I ask, unsure if he'll even sell it to me.

"You could buy regular sage at the grocery, you know." His mouth is turned down into a frown.

"Please?"

He stares at me for a long moment; then he shrugs and rings it up. He wraps the bag in a piece of brown butcher's paper and packages it carefully beside my book.

"Here you go. Now, I don't mean to chase you ladies out, but it's nearly closing time and—"

He doesn't even have the chance to finish kicking us out so he can lock up because Rosemary comes flying up the aisle with Sage's dress bag in one hand and both mugs in the other. She places the dirty mugs on the counter with a clatter and grabs my arm.

"Come on, we have to go!"

"Thank you," I call over my shoulder as I snatch my bag from the counter as she pulls me toward the door.

"Hurry up, Trina just locked the front door. She headed down the alley to the employee parking lot. We have to catch her before she drives off."

I have to trot in order to keep up with her speed-walking pace.

"Mizz Lyman!" she calls out to a woman who's about to turn out of the alley into a paved lot. She stops under a streetlight and turns toward us with a wary expression.

When we're about twenty feet away, she recognizes us. She smiles and her shoulders relax.

"Thyme, Rosemary. What are you girls doing wandering around over here?"

"Just a little shopping." I lift the bag from the bookstore to prove it.

She nods uncertainly and shifts her gaze toward the dress bag in Rosemary's arms.

"Is that Sage's gown?"

"Yep. Denise rescued it and asked us to deliver it to Sage."

She scans the alley behind us. "Denise is with you? I thought she had a meeting."

"She does. She gave us a lift to the bookstore. Victor and Dave are picking us up."

She nods as if she understands, even though I can barely follow our involved travel arrangements myself.

"So, can I ... do something for you?" Her tone is friendly, but her eyes drift over to the parking lot. She clearly wants to get in her car and go home after a long day of work.

"Um ..." I begin.

"Why did you ask your sister to get you the keys to Roman's car?" Rosemary asks in a firm, even tone, just like she said she would.

Trina Lyman's right eyebrow nearly hits her hairline. "Excuse me? What business is it of yours?"

Rosemary shifts her weight and plants her left hand on her hip. "It's our business because your sister gave you *our* sister's keys."

Roman's mom reaches into her jacket pocket and takes out a ring of keys. She flips it through the air toward Rosemary, who catches it one-handed.

"There you go. I'm done with them anyway."

"Right, because you already sto—"

I bring my foot down hard on top of Rosemary's, cutting her

off *and* getting my revenge for the foot-stomping I suffered back at the restaurant.

She glares at me then turns to her left to see who Trina and I are looking at. The man from the bookstore is across the alley, locking up the rear entrance. He waves at Roman's mom.

"Everything okay, Trina?"

"Sure thing, Clovis," she calls back. She flicks her eyes toward us and turns back to him. "These are my future daughter-in-law's sisters, just saying good night." Now she turns to face us. "Goodnight, girls."

The dismissal in her voice is unmistakable. Clovis from the bookstore is watching us closely. I spot several red flannel root bags peeking out from the top of his canvas book tote.

"Goodnight, Mrs. Lyman. We'll see you tomorrow," Rosemary says.

"We will?" I ask.

"Yeah, Sage wants to go to the archeological dig event Denise was talking about. She mentioned it when you were getting your pedicure."

"You'll see to it that Sage gets those keys?" Trina asks.

"Yes, ma'am."

There's nothing left to say, so I drag Rosemary backward up the alley for a few feet. Eventually, she relents and turns around. She calls the guys to tell them we're ready to go and we cross the road to wait for them on a wrought-iron bench in front of a small tot lot playground that fronts a preschool building.

It's full dark now. The shadows are long, and the night air is chilled. I shiver in my thin cardigan. I take my new book from my bag and start to flip through the pages aimlessly, scanning the chapter heading by the light of the streetlamp.

A car drives up the alley, its headlights washing over us, and turns right. It comes to a stop a few yards away at the red light, and Rosemary inhales and digs her nails into my forearm.

"Look!"

I raise my head. Trina Lyman and Clovis from the bookstore are in the car. She's driving, and he's kissing her neck. She throws back her head and laughs, open-mouthed. The light turns green and they drive off.

"So? She has a boyfriend. Good for her."

"Have you ever heard Roman or Sage mention anything about her being in a relationship?"

"No, but it's hardly our business. She's in her fifties, Rosemary. She's allowed to have a private relationship."

Sometimes Rosemary can be just the teensiest bit judgmental.

She shakes her head. "I wonder about you sometimes, Thyme. Look at your bookstore bag. What does it say?"

I read the words printed on the side of the bag. "Frogmore Books and Coffee. Clovis Davis, Proprietor." I look up at her. "Clovis *Davis?* As in the Davis-Lyman feud?"

She purses her lips. "*Mm-hmm.* Could be."

"Roman's mom is fooling around with a Davis? And, Rosemary, he's a root doctor. Or, at least, I think he is."

Her eyes go wide. "What makes you say that?"

"All those little red bags at the store are root bags. For, you know, hoodoo."

We stare at each other for a few seconds. Then the rental car comes to a stop at the curb, and Victor grins at me from the driver's seat. Rosemary picks up Sage's wedding gown and gestures for Victor to pop the trunk. I stick my book back into my bag and help her get the garment bag spread out in the trunk. She slams the lid shut and I follow her into the car.

"What are we going to do?" I whisper as we climb into the back seat.

"Beats the hell out of me," she whispers back.

CHAPTER 23

Rosemary

*W*hen we get to Sage's place, I confirm she hasn't had any muscle relaxants then suggest a nightcap.

She's giddy with excitement at the sight of the heavy white bag that holds her wedding gown. Thyme helps her stow the dress in her closet while I uncork a bottle of red I unearthed from the back of the pantry.

Dave hoists himself up onto the kitchen counter and stares steadily at me. I pretend not to notice.

"Hey, Victor, could you get some glasses down?" I call to Victor, who's paging through the book Thyme bought.

Roman hurries over. "I'll do it. Do you want me to cut up some fruit or something? There's not much here, but we could probably scare up a snack."

"I don't think anyone's going to have much of an appetite," I tell him grimly.

He shoots me a puzzled look and turns to Dave, who shrugs, palms up.

Sage and Thyme return from the bedroom. Thyme gives me a wide-eyed look. Then she jerks her head toward Sage.

Yeah, I'm working on it.

I pass out the wine glasses, reach into my pocket, and take out Sage's set of keys to Roman's car and apartment. I place them on the kitchen counter.

"First my dress, now my keys? Where did you find them?" Sage squeals.

Her excitement makes my heart squeeze. She's not going to like what comes next.

I take a long drink and cut my eyes toward Roman.

"Roman's mom had them."

"My mom? I don't understand."

Thyme pipes up. "Your Aunt Denise said your mom asked her to get them. She said she needed them for a surprise or … something."

Roman's puzzled expression deepens. "Was my mom at Aunt Denise's?"

Thyme coughs.

"No. Actually, we ran into her when we were leaving that bookstore right across the street from where she works," I say.

Sage places her wineglass down on the table with extreme care. She pauses for a moment with her eyes lowered. When she lifts her head and speaks, her voice is dangerously soft. "Rosemary, did you go to Frogmore to harass Trina?"

"We went to the bookstore."

"Uh-huh. And?"

Thyme inches closer to me. "And we had some coffee. And I bought a book … and a present for you. Look!"

She digs the red pouch out of the bookstore bag and thrusts it at Sage, who turns it in her hand, studying it.

"What is it?"

"That's a root bag," Roman tells her.

"A root bag? Like a charm?"

"Yeah."

Thyme interjects, "But it's not a charm. It's not mixed up or whatever you have to do. It's just straight sage."

"You bought me a bag full of sage? Did you get yourself some thyme?" Sage's slow boil seems to have stalled as a result of Thyme's nutty gesture. She even throws me a *she's got to be kidding* look.

I grin and shrug.

"No, it's not *just* because of your name. Did you know it's used to ward off misfortune? Oh, and to reverse spells!" Thyme chirps.

"Really? Where'd you hear that?" Victor wants to know.

"Clovis Davis, the bookseller, told me."

Roman clenches his fists and the veins on the sides of his neck bulge out. "Clovis Davis is a conjurer. And a Davis. You don't want that bag, Sage."

A look passes between me and Thyme. The guys don't notice, but Sage does.

"What?"

"Nothing."

"Just tell me already."

"It just doesn't seem that Roman's mom shares his opinion about Mr. Davis. She gave him a ride home. And they seemed awfully … close."

"Close how?"

"What kind of close?"

"The kissing kind."

"That's a lie!" Roman insists.

"No, it really happened. We saw them at the stoplight. She was driving, and he leaned over and nuzzled her neck. And he had a whole tote bag full of those red root bags, too," Thyme says in a gentle voice.

A heavy hush falls over the room. Dave and Victor are both studiously avoiding meeting anyone's eyes. Roman's fuming.

Thyme's doing her breathing exercise. And Sage is staring straight at me.

"Connect the dots for me," she says. She picks up her glass and takes a drink without taking her eyes off me.

"I think you know."

"Humor me."

I hold her gaze. "If someone's trying to ruin your wedding, it's Roman's mom. And she's working with a Davis to do it."

CHAPTER 24

Sage

After I ask my sisters and their men to leave with a promise to meet them early to go over to St. Helena Island together in the morning, I try to get Roman to talk to me. But it's a lost cause. He goes outside and sits on the balcony in the dark, staring glumly at nothing.

I can't imagine what he's thinking. Is he upset because his mother apparently dislikes me so much she's willing to work with a Davis to derail our wedding? Or is he freaking out because his mom has a boyfriend? Or maybe he's ruminating over my sisters and the way they inappropriately insert themselves into our personal business. The list of possibilities stretches out like a bleak scroll in my mind.

I wish I could call my mom or my dad. But it's after lights out at both of their facilities.

I could go over to Muffy's and see if she's still awake. Except I'm pretty sure Roman wouldn't like it if I aired his mom's dirty laundry to his dad's wife. I laugh at the absurdity of it all.

Then my laughter fades away, and I can feel tears building

behind my eyes, so I grab the book Thyme left behind in her hurry to get out of here before the tension got any worse. It's a history of hoodoo in Beaufort County and the South Carolina Sea Islands. I flip to the back and run my finger along the index, scanning the entries.

When I get to *Davis, Augustus,* I locate the page numbers where his name appears. According to the book, he was a respected conjurer who did root work and spell work on his family farm. The locals called him "Dr. Raven." A photograph in the right column showed a strong, serious-looking man with a piercing gaze. I read on:

Although local lore credits Mr. Davis with these powers, whispers abound that the real conjurer in his home was not Augustus, but his beautiful wife Ginia. No written evidence exists of Ginia Davis's spell work or root work. But it is known that her children and her children's children carried on the traditional ways. Her great-grandson, Clovis Davis, insists that Grandmother Ginia taught his father everything that he subsequently passed down to Clovis and his siblings.

I close the book softly. So Clovis Davis is a direct descendant of the man who broke Roman's Great-Aunt Betsy's heart. And Roman's mom is dating him? Would she really?

I stand up, determined to go outside and make Roman talk to me whether he likes it or not. But he's already on his way inside. He slides the door shut and locks it, neatly sidestepping the bookcase to his left like a reasonably competent human being would.

I cross the room and wrap my arms around his back. I tilt my head back and look up into his sad, tired face. The amber light that usually sparkles in his eyes is dim.

"You doing okay?"

He shrugs.

"Talk to me."

"I was just thinking ... I don't know what my mom's up to. And I know I have to talk to her about the car keys, but she can't be causing everything. The woman who broke the bottle tree, that wasn't my mother. She was at work when that happened."

"That's true," I agree. I stand on my tiptoes and take his face in my hands. After a moment, I say "What about her relationship with Clovis Davis? Are you okay with that?"

"Your sisters are confused. They have to be."

"What if they aren't?"

He doesn't answer. Instead he yawns widely. "It's been one helluva day. And we promised Granny and Aunt Denise we'd be at that archeological thing tomorrow morning. Can we please just go to bed. All our troubles will still be here when the sun comes up. We can worry about this mess after a good night's sleep. What do you say?" His tone is light, but his eyes are pleading.

"Sure. One last question, though."

"You got it." He grabs my hands and holds them between his.

"Do you still want to marry me if your mom hates me?"

He shakes his head. "My mother adores you. But yes, even if she's skulking all over the islands laying curses on us and unleashing evil haints, I still want to marry you. I want it more than I've ever wanted anything, Sage. I love you."

My heart eases, and a smile blooms on my lips. "Okay."

"Just okay?" he teases.

I brush my lips across his. "Let's go to bed and I'll show you how okay it is."

"Lead the way, tiger. Just take it easy with your stitches, okay? The last thing we need to cap off this miserable day is another trip to the emergency room."

"Fair point. I'll just recline against a pile of pillows. You can do all the work."

He emits a fake growl from deep in his throat and scoops me up into his arms. Then he stalks toward the bedroom while I bury my face in his chest and giggle.

CHAPTER 25

Thyme

*A*fter Sage kicks us out, we drive back to the bed and breakfast in awkward silence.

The tension is simmering between Rosemary and Dave. And Victor's doing that tuneless humming thing that makes me slightly stabby.

"So," Dave clears his throat. "When are you two gonna get hitched?"

"Soon," Victor says.

At the same time, I say, "We're not in a hurry."

Rosemary starts laughing so hard it triggers a coughing fit. Dave pounds her on the back. Victor and I shoot each other mortified looks.

When she finally catches her breath, Rosemary gasps, "I'm sorry. It's not funny. It's just … Dave was so desperate to change the subject to something less touchy and look what he went and did."

For his part, Dave doesn't seem to be any more amused than I am. "Sorry, guys. I just sort of thought …"

"So did I." Victor's gripping the steering wheel so tightly that the skin around his knuckles is turning white.

I reach over and cover his hand with mine. "I love you. You know that." I turn and look at Rosemary and Dave. "But my sisters don't exactly have the best track records when it comes to weddings. Why would I want to rush into that kind of drama?"

In the back seat, Rosemary bristles. "Hey! The planning may get kind of hairy, but the wedded bliss part is what counts. Right?"

"Definitely." Dave wraps an arm around her shoulder and hugs her. She snuggles into his side. He kisses her on the cheek and leans forward. "You could always elope, you know."

Believe me, it's not like I haven't thought of it. I steal a glance at Victor. He's frowning thoughtfully. "The idea's not without appeal," he muses. "But it wouldn't be the same without our families there."

"Even my dysfunctional sisters?"

"I'm right here," Rosemary calls from the back.

"Especially your dysfunctional sisters."

We all laugh then, and the knot of anxiety in the pit of my stomach loosens.

"Let's get through Sage and Roman's wedding first," I suggest.

Victor reaches over and grabs my hand. He rubs my fingers. "From your lips to God's ear."

We fall silent again. I can't stop thinking about the look on Roman's face when we told him his mom was getting cozy with Clovis Davis. I have a feeling tomorrow's going to be every bit as interesting as today was. I lean my head back and close my eyes. I can't wait to get back to New York City, where the people are more predictable than these South Carolinians. Cranky and brusque, sure. But blessedly predictable.

CHAPTER 26

Rosemary

*D*ave, Thyme, Victor and I pile out of the rental car and join the crowd forming on the grounds of the old farm located on the outskirts of Frogmore. According to Sage, the landowner bequeathed the land to the Penn Center because it was believed to have historical significance. The Penn Center is an educational and cultural center where the country's first school for freed slaves once stood, and it's committed to preserving Gullah/Geechee culture.

So this archeological dig is a big deal around town. There's a buzz of excitement rising above the murmured conversations. A band is playing. And vendors and community groups are busy setting up tables to sell goodies and pass out literature.

I spot Denise escorting an older woman from the paved parking lot across the road. Denise is wearing cheerful yellow clamdigger pants and white wide-brimmed hat with a yellow ribbon that matches her pants. The older woman is scowling and smacking Denise's hand away from her elbow.

I poke Thyme. "Look. That has to be Roman's Granny Effie."

We wave at the women.

Effie finally manages to dislodge her daughter's hand as they cross the yard to join us. "You'd think a person couldn't walk. Who do you think taught *you* to walk, little missy," she mutters at her daughter.

Oblivious to her mother's ire—or at least unchastened by it—Denise greets us warmly. After a round of hugs, she introduces us to Effie, who shakes each of our hands and asks us questions that make it clear she'd paid attention when Roman and Sage talked about us and that she's sharp as a tack.

"Where's Sage?" Denise wants to know.

"Um, I think she and Roman are picking up his mom on the way. They should be here soon."

Dave's eyes meet mine and flash the message *I'd love to be a fly on the wall of **that** VW bug.*

I guess they figure it'll be better to get everything out in the open with Trina before they get here. I hope they're right. My stomach's been doing flips all morning just thinking about it.

"Well, there they are," Effie says, nodding her head toward the lot.

Sure enough, Sage and Roman are getting out of Roman's car. They head straight toward us. But there's no sign of Trina.

"Uh-oh," Dave says under his breath.

I squeeze his hand. Sage looks worried but not furious or heartbroken. I take it as a good sign.

"Where's your momma?" Denise demands as soon as they join our cluster.

"Good morning to you, too, Auntie." He bends and kisses his grandmother's cheek before turning back to his aunt.

"But, to answer your question, I don't know where my mom is. We stopped by the house at eight o'clock, just like I said we would, and she wasn't there. Her car was gone. So I guess she'll show up at some point. Or she won't."

His shrug does nothing to lessen the harshness of his words, and I cringe.

Sage slips over to give me and Thyme quick hugs.

"How are you holding up?" I whisper.

"Better than he is."

She smiles wanly and reaches into her oversized straw bag. "Oh, Thyme, you left your book at my place last night."

"Thanks." Thyme takes it and tucks it under her arm. "I'll run it back to the car later."

We all stand there clearing our throats and kicking at the dirt for an endless handful of seconds. Finally, Effie demands, "What in heavens name is going on? Y'all have black thunderclouds over your heads."

We shoot looks around but nobody volunteers to speak.

"Well? Am I gonna have to work a tongue-loosening charm on you lot?"

A sonorous voice rings out from behind me. "I believe that's my area of expertise, Mizz Lyman."

In unison, the eight of us turn our heads to see Roman's mother and Clovis Davis marching grimly toward us over a small rise in the hill. They're holding hands and wearing expressions that makes them look like the pictures of martyrs I've seen in history books. Steely-eyed and resigned.

"Why, Clovis. This is a … surprise." Except for the brief hesitation, there's nothing in Effie's voice that gives so much as a hint that the sight of her daughter walking hand-in-hand with a Davis is anything out of the ordinary.

Denise and Roman, however, don't manage to cover up their shock quite as well. It takes Denise a full ten seconds to realize her mouth is agape and snap it shut.

"Mom. So it's true. You're … in cahoots with *him*."

Trina lifts her chin. "Cahoots? Is that what the kids call being in love these days."

I see Clovis tighten his grip on her hand and give it an

encouraging squeeze, exactly like the one I gave Dave just a minute ago.

"You're in love with Clovis Davis." Denise says it as a statement, not a question.

Her sister answers her anyway. "Yes. I am. We've been seeing each other for months now. Ever since my promotion, when I started closing up the store. I'd go over to the book store to get a cup of tea at the end of the night and we got to talking ..."

"And eventually I worked up the nerve to ask the most beautiful woman on the island to go to the movies with me. And we've been keeping company ever since," Clovis breaks in.

Trina beams at him and pats his cheek. "After Sage's sisters saw us in the car together last night, I decided I'm tired of keeping secrets and tired of hiding my feelings. Clovis and I talked it over this morning, and decided it's time to tell you all. I love him, and I don't give a damn about any old curse."

Denise draws in her breath.

Effie's eyes flash. "You're a grown woman, Katrina Anne. You go on and love anyone you want. But you watch your language."

"Yes, ma'am. I'm sorry, mama."

Clovis clears his throat. "Now. I know the Lymans and the Davises haven't always gotten along"—this gets a snort out of Roman, but Clovis plows ahead, undeterred—"But don't you all think it's time to bury the hatchet? Why, I think it's what Gus and Betsy would want."

I'm beginning to feel awkward, just standing here, watching this family drama play out, so I catch Thyme's eye and tilt my head toward the vendor area to see if she wants to drift away from the group. The frown she gives me in return makes clear her views on this plan.

"And would Gus and Great-Great-Aunt Betsy want you and my mother to try to ruin my wedding?" Roman demands.

Uh-oh. Too late to sneak off now.

Clovis Davis gives Roman a puzzled look. But Trina pulls

herself up to her full height and shakes her finger at her son.

"Are you out of your mind? What are you talking about?"

"Oh, come on, Mom. You've been working against me and Sage this whole time. Did you whisper in Reverend Walker's ear and tell him to cancel on us?"

"What! I never—"

Denise breaks in. "Now, you simmer down, Roman. I told Sage I was gonna talk to Reverend Walker, and I did. I impressed upon him how important it is to the Lymans to have the presiding minister of Second Baptist perform your wedding ceremony, and he reconsidered that invitation to talk to the interfaith conference. He's gonna send Lonnie Reed in his stead."

"You did that? You convinced him?" Sage asks, awe in her voice.

"I surely did. All it took was a peach crumble with fresh whipping cream. I just haven't had a chance to tell you."

"Thank you."

Roman relents. "Okay, well, that was nice. And it was good of you to get Sage's dress back from Mrs. James. Thanks for that." He turns back to his mother, eyes flashing. "But you. Are you going to deny you used Sage's spare key to break into my car and *steal* our wedding rings?"

Trina's face goes rigid but she doesn't answer.

"Yeah, I didn't think so," he goes on.

Finally, she spits the words from between clenched teeth. "Why don't you check your glovebox again, Roman. Do it now. We'll wait."

Mother and son glare at each other for a long, hard moment. Then he turns on his heel and stalks toward the car. Sage watches him, her face pale and drawn. Sweat beads her forehead.

"Are you okay?" I whisper.

She nods unconvincingly.

A second later, Roman's back holding a dark blue velvet double ring box and wearing a bashful expression.

"Go on. Open it," his mother instructs.

He glances at Sage. She holds out her hand and he places the box in her palm. She gently lifts the hinged lid and looks up at Trina, confused.

"But these aren't our rings. They're beautiful, but they're not ours."

I crane my neck for a peek, but the angle's no good.

"No, they're not. They're Gus and Betsy's rings. From the wedding that never happened. I inherited Great-Aunt Betsy's when she passed. And Gus's went to Clovis after his father died. We thought you should have them, so I switched them out with your rings. I took the box from the jewelry store from your car on Wednesday afternoon. I replaced it with these rings inside yesterday morning while you were at the gym."

Clovis clears his throat. "You don't have to use them if you don't want to. But they're yours now."

Sage's eyes fill with tears. "But ... the two of you ... maybe you'll want them in case you get married someday?"

Trina giggles like a teenager. "Honey, we did that already. We went to see the justice of the peace the week before last to make it official. We're having rings made for us. We wanted something with no connection to the past."

"Wait? You're *married?*" Roman's jaw hangs open.

"Yes, son. Like your mother said, about ten days ago we got hitched. We've been slowly moving her things into my place after work. That's why she's been so hard to get a hold of lately—you may have noticed."

"And you didn't tell us?" Denise demands.

"We didn't want to make a big fuss, not while the kids are busy planning their wedding."

"Well, I never ..." Denise begins.

But she stops mid-sentence when Sage sways from side to side, rolls her eyes back into her head, and crumples to the ground in a heap.

CHAPTER 27

Sage

I come to and blink, trying to get my bearings. I'm stretched out across two folding chairs, the fancy wooden kind with the white padded seats. A thin blanket covers me. I push it off and swing my legs around so I'm sitting up.

"Easy."

I turn toward the voice, Effie's voice. She smiles and hands me a glass of orange juice.

"Drink this. It'll help."

I steady my hand and sip the juice.

"Course, my mama always said a pinch of salt on the tongue worked wonders. But they probably don't have any salt around here."

I look around. "Where are we?"

"The old Thompson place. The farmhouse."

"I fainted?" It's starting to come back to me.

"You surely did. Roman carried you up here, and someone scared up a blanket and some juice. Those sisters of yours sure are worried." She leans in conspiratorially. "But I told all the young folks they were making too much noise and shooed them off."

"Why? They weren't bothering me," I point out.

"Roman needs to talk to his mama. And I need to talk to you."

Now I'm wide awake. "Yes, ma'am."

"You've got to convince Roman not to be too hard on Trina for keeping her romance with Clovis a secret. She's been lonely for a while now. First, Roman got that fancy job with Chip and started spending a lot of time on Hilton Head. Then you came into the picture. She likes you, Sage. But she raised that boy all on her own. He's been her life. Now, he's got you and a relationship with Chip. And she had nothing. Until the good Lord brought Clovis into her path."

Even as my heart swells for Trina, my brain's parsing Granny Effie's words.

"Granny?"

"Yes, sugar."

"Did the good Lord bring Clovis into her path—or was it someone else? Maybe someone who matches her hats to her outfits?"

Effie looks at me for a moment. Then she barks out a long laugh. "Child, I knew I liked you. Yes, truth be told, the first night Trina ventured into Clovis' bookstore, I do believe it was because Denise was meeting her there and, wouldn't you know, she 'ran late.'"

"Which she never does."

"Mmm-hmm."

We smile at each other.

"I think I'm okay now, really." I get to my feet just as Thyme comes rushing into the house.

"Oh, good, you're awake! They've found something at the dig site!"

~

THYME AND I help Effie navigate the rutted path from the house to the excavation site. Because we're not her daughters, or perhaps because the uneven ground is tricky to cover, she doesn't slap our hands away.

Roman, Victor, and Dave are huddled around the hole in the earth when we reach the site. Rosemary is off to the side talking to Clovis and Trina.

"Where's Denise?" Effie asks no one in particular.

Trina jerks her head toward a cluster of dark-suited men. Important-looking men. The suits shift and a flash of yellow shines out from their midst.

Roman grins at me and comes walking over.

"Feeling better?"

"Better now."

"They say it was probably just low blood sugar. You need to eat better."

"It's been a long three days," I tell him.

"Four days."

"No wonder it feels so long."

He grins at me, just as Denise emerges from the group of men clutching a tarnished silver frame. She carries it with great care and shows it to her mother.

"Look, Mama, they've found a photograph of Ginia Thompson Davis. Director Charles thought you should see it first since you fought so hard to raise the money for this dig."

Effie peers down at the picture. I look over her shoulder. I immediately recognize the somber Gus Davis from the photograph in Thyme's book. My eyes slide across the image to his wife.

"That's Ginia Davis?"

"Yes," Denise says. "Wasn't she beautiful?"

She was. "She looks just like Hunter Redforth." Doesn't anyone else see it? I mean, the resemblance is beyond striking. I could be looking at Hunter dressed up in period clothing. It's spooky.

"Well, that's not surprising," Trina says, coming over to take a look at the photograph.

"It's not?"

"Of course not. Hunter *is* Ginia's great-granddaughter."

"Pardon?"

Trina gives me a curious smile. "Clovis was married before. He and his wife—"

A memory from the spa surfaces. "Davina," I supply.

"That's right. Clovis and Davina had one daughter, Hunter Alysse. She goes by Hunter now. But when they lived in Frogmore, everyone knew her as Allie."

Allie Davis from Frogmore, the lithe woman who ran from my garden after smashing my spirit tree. Hunter Redforth from Hilton Head, the polished wedding coordinator who was so eager to help me move my wedding off St. Helena. One and the same.

I excuse myself and walk down the hill to the main tent, where the local news stations are setting up to report the find live. I'm pretty sure I'll find Hunter here, where the cameras are. I suspect she's not going to miss a moment in the spotlight. And I'm right.

She sees me from about twenty feet away and flashes me a brilliant smile.

"Sage! What a nice surprise."

"Is it?"

Her eyes flicker warily. "Of course."

"You look just like your great-grandmother. I saw the picture. The resemblance is astonishing."

She lowers her gaze modestly. "I saw it, too. I think Ginia's prettier than I am."

I'm suddenly too tired to play this Southern 'say everything on a slant and passive-aggressively score your points' game. I am, after all, a Jersey girl. And even a homeschooled Jersey girl raised by hippie parents has a fair amount of spunk.

"Why'd you try to ruin my wedding? Because your dad and Roman's mom got together?"

She narrows her eyes for a moment, like she's considering lying, then discards the notion. "No. To tell the truth, I barely know Clovis. My mother and stepfather never wanted me to have a relationship with him. And I don't."

"So, what was it then? Why go after me and Roman? You don't even know me."

"I know enough. I know you have one foot in Hilton Head society and one foot here, an in with the Gullah/Geechee. You, a Yankee, and a white one, to boot. While *I* couldn't even join the Frogmore Ladies' Council. Not considered a native, that's what Denise told me. Because I didn't live on the island for more than twelve years."

"So? You're on every rising star list on Hilton Head. You belong to the Junior League. You're the event coordinator for the most exclusive country club on the island."

She snaps her fingers. "Right, and none of that matters once you cross that bridge to St. Helena. If I can't move in this world, why should you be able to?"

She's jealous. The realization makes me lightheaded all over again.

"That's why you were trying to convince me to get married at the club?"

"Look. You don't belong here. I tried to make you see that by doing little things, canceling your flower order, having Jessalyn's main creditor put her into default so you'd lose your dress. The reverend backing out was just a stroke of luck." She pauses and tips her head to the side. "Or maybe that was Ginia lending a hand. But once you got the idea that the Davis curse was on you, I just decided to run with it."

"You're bananas."

She shrugs. "I'm Ginia Davis' great-granddaughter. And I'm her spiritual heir. I want what I want, and I get it or I get my revenge. It's that simple." She smiles that brilliant, warm smile that makes her seem so approachable, so lovely.

I back away from her, slowly, because it occurs to me, belatedly, that she actually is demented. I wonder how I'm ever going to convince anyone that she's the one who tried to derail the wedding. As I turn the corner, I realize I'm not going to have to.

Just behind the beverage cart, not ten feet away, Clovis Davis is getting mic'ed up for an interview about the discovery of his grandmother's photograph. From the stricken look on his face, he's heard every word.

A moment later, a matching expression of dismay spreads across my face as I realize something else: In three short weeks, the demented wedding-ruiner is going to be my stepsister-in-law.

CHAPTER 28

Three weeks later
The Thompson Historical Homestead,
St. Helena Island

Sage

I stretch out my arms and spin in a slow circle. The long skirt of my wedding gown puddles around my feet in a whorl of ivory silk.

"Well?"

Rosemary nods approvingly. "You're gorgeous. Just try not to trip on your way down the aisle."

Thyme covers her laugh with a cough, but Mom clicks her tongue.

"Stop it, you two. Sage is going to *float* down the aisle, full of grace and ease," MJ assures us all. It even sounds like she believes it.

Muffy, who may be even clumsier than I am, looks up from tying the ribbons on Skylar's dress and winks at me. I figure there's a sixty-percent chance I don't get caught up in the dress and faceplant. Especially considering the 'aisle' is a rough path cut through the field.

"Besides," MJ goes on, "I thought you lifted the curse? *Nothing's* going to go wrong today," she insists.

I can sense she's getting ready to propose we do some positive visualizations—or maybe a round of affirmation chanting. And for all her kookiness, she's right that mindset matters. But we're on a tight schedule here. Time for a distraction.

I traipse over to her and wrap my arms around her. "I'm so glad you're here today, Mom."

She gives me a squeeze. "I wouldn't miss it for the world, darling girl. Oh, wait a minute." She reaches in the pocket of her vintage silk dress. I have to hand it to her, the A-line cut dress suits her *and* she has pockets. Who doesn't love a dress with pockets?

She removes a tissue that's been folded into a small, thick square. I realize I'm holding my breath because she could have just about anything squirreled away in there.

Just please don't be animal bones.

She opens the tissue to reveal a gleaming silver coin. "You have something old—Betsy and Gus's rings. You have something new, I'm sure?"

I gesture at the dress.

"Something borrowed?"

"Yep," Hunter chirps. "She's wearing Ginia's hair comb."

The silver comb was unearthed the same day as the photograph, and Clovis insists it belongs to Hunter now. She had it cleaned and polished until it gleamed and asked me to wear it today. It's perched atop my complicated bun, shining like the sun.

Until now, Hunter's been so quiet, I almost forget she's in the room. But she *is* my future stepsister-in-law and Trina's stepdaughter, now. So once I calmed down and decided not to press charges for her vandalism, she stepped up and helped me whip the wedding into shape.

To her credit, convincing Reverend Walker to perform the ceremony at her great-grandmother's childhood farm instead of the church was a stroke of genius. Everyone'll be more comfortable outside, and the reverend agreed that uniting the Lyman and Davis families and ending the feud on the land where Ginia was born symbolizes a new beginning. As a bonus, my Wiccan mother is unlikely to freak out because there won't be any religious iconography to set her off. Win, win, win.

But Hunter's done more than secure the perfect venue. This wedding is going to be amazing, and it's mainly her doing. She thinks of *everything.*

Mom's nodding her approval. "Something blue?"

"Oh, yeah."

There's so much blue. Hunter's incorporated the shade the Gullah call haint blue into everything from the ribbons on the bouquets to the ballet slipper-style flats on my feet. Just because there aren't any evil spirits currently torturing us is no reason to be lazy about it. We're even using cobalt blue bottles on the tables as vases. Better safe than sorry.

Mom presses the coin into my hand. "There's another verse, you know. The full poem goes something old, something new, something borrowed, something blue, and a lucky sixpence for your shoe."

I examine the disc. It's an actual sixpence.

"Where did you get this?'

"Oh, I've had it forever. My grandmother gave it to me when your dad and I had our handfasting ceremony. It's apparently quite valuable."

"Really?"

"It was minted in the early nineteen hundreds when the coins were more than ninety percent real silver. Or so I'm told."

I kiss her cheek. "Thanks, Mom."

Thyme hurries over to crouch and help me tuck the coin into my shoe. I wiggle my toes. I can't even feel it.

As she stands up, she says, "Mom?" in a careful voice.

Mom smiles, already anticipating the question. "Yes, Thyme, I disclosed it as an asset during the forfeiture proceeding. But that snotty IRS lady scoffed at a penny, and a foreign one at that. So, they didn't want it. I'm minding my ps and qs, girls."

Thyme's mouth curves into a relieved smile. "Good. We want you and Dad to be released early with credit for good behavior."

Mom pinches her cheek. "So do I. I'm sure I'll have another wedding to attend soon."

The barest shadow flits across Thyme's face. It vanishes so quickly, I wonder if I imagined it.

Trina appears in the doorway. "Y'all ready? Everyone's here. And, truth be told, we better get this started before Roman faints. That boy is jumpier than a grasshopper." She gives me a wide grin.

Knowing Roman's nervous, too, somehow calms my jangled nerves. Rosemary hands me my bouquet and squeezes my arm. "Showtime."

I take a deep breath and I sweep my way out of the room.

DAD TUCKS my arm under his elbow and flashes me a grin. He doesn't say anything, but the tremulous smile says it all. He's always been the most sentimental of the Fields. He's holding back tears. I stretch up onto my toes and give him a peck beside his ear.

"Love you, Dad."

He pats my hand and makes a choking sound.

The first, sweet notes of the Second Baptist choir's a cappella arrangement of Roman's favorite hymn, "Be Still," rise on the air, and Rosemary hooks her arm through Thyme's. They start down the aisle between the two sections of padded seats. The choir was all Denise's idea. And Clovis arranged for a Zydeco band to play at the reception. Apparently, he's in a book club with the washboard player.

When my sisters asked if they could escort each other down the aisle, I said yes immediately. Who wants to take that interminable walk all alone, with all those eyes staring at you? Skylar apparently is up for the job, though.

I watch her counting, mouthing the numbers, as Rosemary and Thyme pass the first three rows. When they reach the fourth, she shoots me an excited grin and steps forward with her basket of sweetgrass roses, picked from Muffy's garden just this morning.

The way the wedding's evolved into a project that interweaves my family, the Lymans, the Moores, and the Davises makes my heart swell and my eyes fill. I blink down at the flowers in my hand to stop the tears. My eyes fall on the sage leaves tucked into the bouquet for luck and I take one more deep, centering breath.

The choir's last note hangs in the air, and the afternoon is still for one crystalline moment. I see Dave and Victor standing side by side with Dylan straight as a soldier in front of them. And next to them, Roman. His amber eyes are locked on me. His angular face serious, but his mouth soft and full. A slow smile starts at his lips and spreads to his eyes.

Someone, at this point I don't even know who, begins to play the violin. I move forward toward Roman as if I'm being pulled by an invisible ribbon, tying me to him for all time. And, literally, the rest of the ceremony is a blur of emotion.

Twenty minutes later, I'm in Roman's arms and he's crushing his mouth against mine, covering my lips with a strong, long kiss. So, apparently we said our vows and exchanged rings and Reverend Walker pronounced us husband and wife. I really hope Chip's videographer captured the entire thing, because I'd love to know what happened.

Reverend Walker beams and spreads his arms wide. The whooping, cheering, and clapping intensify. I stare down at Betsy

Lyman's never-worn wedding band on my finger in amazement. Then Roman squeezes my hand.

"Ready?"

Ready for what? The rest of our lives? Sure.

I lift my eyes to see that the question wasn't rhetorical. Hunter's hustling up the aisle clutching a creamy white broom decorated with blooms and ribbons.

I'd forgotten this part was coming. One last chance for Sage to fall on her newly-wedded face in front of two hundred people.

Hunter crouches and places the broom in our path. Reverend Walker booms, "Roman and Sage will now jump the broom."

I grip Roman's hand. We swing our hands back and forth, *one, two, three.* Dylan and Skylar are already clapping excitedly as their big brother and I leap over the broom and into our new life together.

I land on my feet and Reverend Walker says, "Let's get this celebration started!"

There's a chorus of *hallelujahs,* and we set off down the aisle.

THE RECEPTION STRETCHES LATE into the night. Hundreds of candles light the field and the Zydeco band keeps our guests on their feet, hopping and singing. It turns out Victor has some moves. He and Thyme are a big hit on the dance floor.

Rosemary and Dave are deep in conversation with Hunter and her date. Rosemary must be telling one of her stories, because the others are throwing back their heads with open-mouthed laughter and wiping tears from their eyes when they catch their breath.

Roman and I sit at the sweetheart table, our fingers entwined, and watch. Every so often we'll take a bite of Rosemary's unbelievably delicious honeysuckle lavender cake with lemon cream.

It sounds like hyperbole to call a dessert a masterpiece, but if anything, it's an understatement.

I make sure we each also nibble on Trina's sesame seed benne wafers. Most of the buttery, nutty cookies are going home with our guests in blue favor bags, but the wafers are supposed to bring luck to a marriage. Also, they pair nicely with champagne, so I made us up a plate.

Roman nods toward the parents' table, where Muffy and Chip, Trina and Clovis, and Mary Jane and Bart are chatting away. "What on earth do you think those six are talking about?"

The question boggles my mind. I can almost feel my synapses straining as my brain fumbles for an answer to this unanswerable question.

Finally, I shake my head and smile. "Could be anything. Literally, anything, from hoodoo curses to the performance of the stock market to how to smuggle a shank into prison."

He grins at me. "Nah. Easy money says they're jawing about when we're going to give them grandkids."

My eyes fly open and I turn my head to the empty table for two set up just next to ours. I take in the two uneaten plates of food, the dish of benne wafers, the two undrunk glasses of wine, the flickering candle, and the blue cobalt vase of cream-colored roses.

I implore the thin air near the table, "Do you hear that Gus and Betsy? We need your protection."

Roman laughs and pulls me close. "They can't help us now. That's a nice touch—your mom's idea of inviting their spirits to our wedding."

I snuggle closer to him as the breeze picks up. "It is. I feel like maybe we've given them the wedding they never had."

The wind dances over the blue glass bottles on our table and the tables around us, and a faint, low rumble sounds, as if Gus is agreeing. I raise my eyes to Roman's, and I can tell he hears it, too.

THANK YOU!

Thanks for reading *Wedding Bells and Hoodoo Spells!* The sisters' adventures continue in *Wanted Wed or Alive*, available now!

Keep reading. You can always find an up-to-date list of the titles in this series, as well as the books in my other series, on my website, www.melissafmiller.com.

Sign up. While you're at my website, sign up for my email newsletter to be the first to know when I have a new release. In addition to new release alerts, subscribers receive notices of sales and other book news, goodies, and exclusive subscriber bonuses.

Review it. I'd love it if you'd head back to where you bought this book and consider posting a short review to help other readers decide whether they might enjoy it.

ABOUT THE AUTHOR

USA Today bestselling author Melissa F. Miller was born in Pittsburgh, Pennsylvania. Although life and love led her to Philadelphia, Baltimore, Washington, D.C., and, ultimately, South Central Pennsylvania, she secretly still considers Pittsburgh home.

In college, she majored in English literature with concentrations in creative writing poetry and medieval literature and was stunned, upon graduation, to learn that there's not exactly a job market for such a degree. After working as an editor for several years, she returned to school to earn a law degree. She was that annoying girl who loved class and always raised her hand. She practiced law for fifteen years, including a stint as a clerk for a federal judge, nearly a decade as an attorney at major international law firms, and several years running a two-person law firm with her lawyer husband.

Now, powered by coffee, she writes legal thrillers and homeschools her three children. When she's not writing, and some-times when she is, Melissa travels around the country in an RV with her husband, her kids, and her cat.

Connect with me:
www.melissafmiller.com